INVISIBLE FIENDS

THE BEAST

D0332817

INVISIBLE

FIENDS

THE BEAST

HarperCollins *Children's Books*

First published in Great Britain by
HarperCollins *Children's Books* 2012

HarperCollins *Children's Books* is a division of HarperCollins*Publishers* Ltd,
77–85 Fulham Palace Road, Hammersmith, London W6 8JB

The HarperCollins *Children's Books* website address is
www.harpercollins.co.uk

1

ISBN 978-0-00-731518-5

Printed and bound in England by Clays Ltd, St Ives plc

MIX
Paper from
responsible sources
FSC
www.fsc.org   FSC™ C007454

For me old mucker, Tommy Donbavand, aka Wobblebottom.

Sorry for nailing you to that ceiling in the last book.

PROLOGUE

What had I expected to see? I wasn't sure. An empty street. One or two late-night wanderers, maybe. But not this. Never this.

There were hundreds of them. *Thousands*. They scuttled and scurried through the darkness, swarming over the village like an infection; relentless and unstoppable.

I leaned closer to the window and looked down at the front of the hospital. One of the larger creatures was tearing through the fence, its claws slicing through the wrought-iron bars as if they were cardboard. My breath fogged the glass and the monster vanished behind a cloud of condensation. By the time the pane cleared the *thing* would be inside the hospital. It would be up the stairs in moments. Everyone in here was as good as dead.

The distant thunder of gunfire ricocheted from somewhere near the village centre. A scream followed – short and sharp, then suddenly silenced. There were no more gunshots after that, just the triumphant roar of something sickening and grotesque.

I heard Ameena take a step closer behind me. I didn't need to look at her reflection in the window to know how terrified she was. The crack in her voice said it all.

'It's the same everywhere,' she whispered.

I nodded, slowly. 'The town as well?'

She hesitated long enough for me to realise what she meant. I turned away from the devastation outside. 'Wait... You really mean *everywhere*, don't you?'

Her only reply was a single nod of her head.

'*Liar!*' I snapped. It couldn't be true. This couldn't be happening.

She stooped and picked up the TV remote from the

day-room coffee table. It shook in her hand as she held it out to me.

'See for yourself.'

Hesitantly, I took the remote. 'What channel?'

She glanced at the ceiling, steadying her voice. 'Any of them.'

The old television set gave a faint *clunk* as I switched it on. In a few seconds, an all-too-familiar scene appeared.

Hundreds of the creatures. Cars and buildings ablaze. People screaming. People running. People *dying*.

Hell on Earth.

'That's New York,' she said.

Click. Another channel, but the footage was almost identical.

'London.'

Click.

'I'm... I'm not sure. Somewhere in Japan. Tokyo, maybe?'

It could have been Tokyo, but then again it could have been anywhere. I clicked through half a dozen more channels, but the images were always the same.

'It happened,' I gasped. 'It actually happened.'

I turned back to the window and gazed out. The clouds above the next town were tinged with orange and red. It was already burning. They were destroying everything, just like *he'd* told me they would.

This was it.

The world was ending.

Armageddon.

And it was all my fault.

THREE DAYS EARLIER...

Chapter One

THE NIGHT BUS

I woke up screaming. This, of late, was not unusual.

The seats beneath me creaked in complaint as I sat upright and tried to shake away the memories of the nightmares before they could fully take hold. No such luck.

The faces of the fiends I'd fought leered at me – vague, half-formed shapes tormenting me from the deepest recesses of my own mind:

Caddie, make-up smeared across her bone-white skin.

The Crowmaster, his empty eye sockets alive with maggots.

Doc Mortis, scalpel in hand, blood spattered across his filthy white coat.

Other images, too. The blubbery remains of the dead man on the train; Marion's flesh-stripped skeleton; my mum, unconscious on a hospital bed.

For a long time I'd tried to resist them, to fill my brain with other thoughts until there was no room left for monsters and horror. It never worked. If anything, it just prolonged the whole ordeal. I'd eventually learned not to fight them, to let them wash over me instead, paying them as little attention as possible.

So there, in the darkness, I closed my eyes, sat still, pulled the collar of my stolen coat tighter around my neck, and let the monsters do their worst.

Several minutes later, I blinked my eyes open. I spent a few more seconds steadying my breath, watching it roll from my mouth as shaky white clouds. Only then did I begin to pay attention to my surroundings.

It was dark, but then it was January and it was early. I never slept late any more. I was on the back seat of a bus that was parked up at the depot. We'd been sleeping here for the last few nights. Not the same bus every time, but the same depot, sneaking through a hole in the fence long after the place had been locked up for the night.

We took it in turns sleeping on the back seat. It was a padded bench, designed to take five or six passengers. This made it much longer than the other seats, and so more comfortable to sleep on. Not *comfortable*, but *more* comfortable.

Last night had been my night up the back, so tonight I'd be on one of the two-seaters. I was dreading it already.

'Ameena.'

Her name came out as a whisper of white mist. Sometimes, my early-morning screaming fit would wake her up, but more and more often these days she was able to sleep through it. Maybe she was getting used to it, or maybe she was just too tired to respond. Either way, she hadn't reacted this morning.

'Ameena,' I said again, louder this time. It was too early for anyone to be at the depot, but there was still part of me that was too afraid to talk at normal volume, in case it attracted attention. Ameena had laughed when

I'd told her that. Everything we'd been through, and I was scared of a telling off from a bus driver.

I didn't want to risk raising my voice any more, so I took hold of the cold metal handle on the back of the seat in front and leaned over it.

'Ameena?'

No. Not Ameena. Not anyone.

I looked to the seat across the aisle. Empty. I looked along the aisle itself, squinting through the gloom. No shape curled up on the floor. No legs stretched out across the gap. No signs of life anywhere.

I'd woken up alone. This was very unusual.

We'd been on the run for two weeks. Well, technically I'd been on the run, and Ameena had just been keeping me company. The police thought I'd killed my mum's cousin. They also thought I'd attacked my mum, beating her so violently she'd been left in a coma, barely clinging to life.

I hadn't done either of them. But I'd confessed to both.

Long story.

I'd had to fake taking Ameena hostage to get past the police at the hospital. Amazingly, it had worked, and we'd managed to get away without being caught.

For days afterwards, our faces were all over the newspapers. The TV too, probably, although I hadn't exactly had time to tune in. We'd kept moving, never settling in one place for long, sleeping in alleyways and in doorways and, on one particularly stormy night, a bus shelter.

It was the bus shelter that had given Ameena the idea of finding the bus depot. We'd been spending the night there ever since, going to sleep together every night, and waking up together every morning.

Until today.

'Ameena.'

I said her name again, more for the comfort of hearing it spoken out loud than anything else. She wasn't on the bus, and that raised one very obvious question: where was she?

The windows were thick with frost, making it impossible

to see anything but the hazy glow of the streetlights on the pavement beyond the depot fence. There was nothing else for it. If Ameena wasn't on the bus, I'd have to go out and find her.

Go outside.

In the dark.

Alone.

Recent events told me this probably wasn't a great idea, but what choice did I have? Had I been the one missing, Ameena wouldn't hesitate before coming to find me. I owed her the same, at least.

I headed for the door, checking each row of seats, hoping I'd find her curled up on one of them, snoring softly. By the time I made it to the front, all my hopes were dashed.

She was out *there* somewhere, and I had no idea where or why. I pulled my coat tighter, took a steadying breath, and reached for the door.

Before my fingers were anywhere near it, the door opened noisily, folding inwards like a concertina. I stepped back, tripping over the step and landing heavily on the floor as a figure stepped from the darkness, bringing with it a cloud of cold, frosty air.

'Morning, kiddo,' Ameena said. Her teeth were chattering as she pushed the door closed and held up a flimsy white carrier bag. 'Say hello to breakfast.'

I ran my finger along the inside of the plastic sandwich-pack, scooping up the last few stray crumbs. We'd had half the sandwich each, washed down by swigs from a one-litre carton of milk.

Only when we'd finished the lot did I ask where it had come from.

'Petrol station,' Ameena replied, crushing the milk carton and stuffing it back in the now-empty bag. 'Found some money on the floor when I was going to sleep. Thought I'd give us a treat.'

I suspected Ameena wasn't telling me the whole truth, but I wasn't about to start asking questions. The sandwich had been the only thing I'd eaten in the last 24 hours, and I was beyond caring where or how she'd managed to get her hands on it.

'I was worried,' I admitted. 'Thought someone had...' I left the sentence hanging there, not quite sure what I'd thought had happened to her.

'Kidnapped me?' she said.

I nodded. 'Yeah.'

'Murdered me?'

'Well...'

'Fed me to their evil crow army?'

I shrugged. 'Maybe.'

She shook her head. 'Nope. Just buying sandwiches.'

'Right,' I said. 'That's OK then.'

We were both on the back seat, facing each other, our feet almost touching. She slid backwards and leaned against the window. I did the same, then leaned forward again when the frosty glass began to bite at me through the thin coat.

'So, what's the plan for today? Some fine dining? A shopping spree?' Ameena asked. 'Roaming the streets for hours, then legging it every time we see a cop? The decision, Mr Alexander, is you—'

'I want to go home.'

'Oh. Right.' She blinked, and I could almost hear her brain processing this information. 'I dunno...'

'I just...' I lowered my head and looked at my hands. They were knotted together for warmth, so I couldn't tell which fingers belonged to which hand. 'We won't stay long. I just... I want to see it.'

It was Ameena's turn to lean forward. 'She won't be there,' she said, her voice taking on a soft edge she hardly ever used. 'Your mum. The papers said she was still in the—'

'I know,' I said quickly. 'I know that. But that was three days ago, and it's...' I untangled my hands and stared down at my open palms. 'I just need to see it.'

'It's a long way.' Ameena looked around at the inside of the bus. 'And we've got it good here. Roof over our head. Something to sleep on. It could be a lot worse.'

I didn't say anything. Ameena wasn't going for the idea, I could tell.

'Of course, we could have it even better,' she continued, 'if someone would use his magic powers to—'

'Stop it,' I said flatly. 'They're not *magic powers*. And I told you already, I'm not using them again. Not unless it's an emergency.'

'But you could—'

'We don't *know* what I could do!' I snapped, and I realised I was standing up now, glaring down at her.

I'd first discovered my "magic powers" while fighting Mr Mumbles. It started with an itchy tingling across my scalp. Next thing I knew, things I imagined started to become real. I'd used the power to defeat Mr Mumbles, but I'd since found out that it was more dangerous than I could've guessed.

'The Crowmaster told me that every time I use my, my... *abilities*, I'm playing right into my dad's hands.'

'The Crowmaster said a lot of things,' Ameena shrugged. 'Don't think he was the most trustworthy of sources, to be honest.'

'Well, I'm not taking the chance. Not unless there's no other choice,' I replied, lowering my voice again. 'My dad told me that one day I'd help him kill everyone on Earth, and I don't want to risk proving him right.'

Ameena shook her head, then gave another half-hearted shrug. 'Suit yourself,' she said. 'But you *could* just conjure us up a cake or something. I mean, it's not like anyone's ever been killed by a French Fancy.'

I opened my mouth to argue, but then saw the smirk playing at the corners of her mouth.

'Shut up,' I said, smiling on the inside, if not the outside. 'So, are we going home or what?'

Down at the front of the bus, the door slid open with a soft *hiss*. We ducked at the same time, dropping to the floor behind a row of seats. The bus dipped to the left a little as someone heavy climbed inside.

Ameena mouthed something to me from the other side of the aisle. I had absolutely no idea what it was, so I just shrugged in reply. She shrugged back, leaving me even more confused than I had been. As I tried to guess what she'd said, the door of the bus hissed closed.

There was silence for a moment, before footsteps clacked along the aisle, slow and steady, like the ticking of an old clock. With every step the floor beneath us gave a slight shake. The vibrations got worse as the steps drew closer and closer, until...

'Ruddy Nora!'

The voice was sharp and panicked. I looked up into the wobbly face of a grey-haired man. 'Oi!' he cried. 'Who are...? What are...? Why...?' His voice trailed off. 'Oi!' he said again, although you could tell his heart wasn't in it this time.

Ameena stood up first. I was a second or two behind her. The man took a step backwards, eyeing us nervously. He was slightly shorter than Ameena, a little taller than me, wider than both of us combined. He wore a light blue shirt with a dark blue tie and a badge identifying him as "Dave Morgan, Driver".

'What are you doing here?' he asked, his eyes constantly flitting between us. 'You shouldn't be in here.'

'Says who?' Ameena demanded.

'Sorry,' I said quickly. Ameena had a lot of strengths, but diplomacy wasn't one of them. 'We didn't... It was freezing. We didn't have anywhere else to go.'

Dave Morgan, Driver, kept his gaze on me. 'What,' he began, 'you homeless or something?'

I nodded.

'Bloody Hell,' he mumbled. His round shoulders seemed to sag. 'How old are you?'

'Thirteen,' I told him.

His eyes opened wide. *Thirteen? And you're...*' He shook his head. To his credit, he looked genuinely concerned. 'Bloody Hell. That's not right. That's not right, that. There must be somewhere you can go?'

Neither of us replied.

'We could get you to the police,' he suggested. 'They'll find a—'

'No!' Ameena and I both said it at the same time. The driver must've heard something in our voices, or spotted something in our eyes, because he took another step back, suddenly suspicious. He looked at Ameena for a long time, then back to me. A flicker of a frown crossed his face.

'Wait a minute,' he said, his eyes narrowing. 'I know you. You're them kids from the news, aren't you?' He glared at me. 'You're the one what killed that woman.'

Ameena swung out from behind the seat, slamming her shoulder into the driver's bulging belly before he had a chance to react. He stumbled backwards, then thudded down on to a seat as Ameena gave him a sideways shove.

'Barney!' he bellowed, his fat fingers grabbing for Ameena. 'Barney, get in here!'

He moved to get up, but Ameena pushed him back down. 'Don't just stand there!' she cried, shooting me one of her looks. '*Leg it!*'

Chapter Two

THIS OLD HOUSE

I did as I was told, racing along the aisle, bounding over the driver's legs, then hurrying to where Ameena was already opening the door. She jumped the steps, landing silently on the ground. I leapt after her, then yelped as my feet slid in opposite directions on the icy road surface.

Ameena caught me by the wrist, pulling me up and on through the grey, early-morning light. We ran along the side of our bus and sped down a narrow alleyway between two more parked coaches.

'Barney!' We could still hear the driver shouting. 'Barney, where are you?'

A shape, impossible to make out clearly, moved through

the gloom up ahead of us. Ameena ducked low and we froze, waiting for whoever it was to pass.

'Come on,' she urged when the coast was clear. We continued through the maze of parked coaches, keeping low. When we finally reached the last bus, Ameena poked her head out and looked around. The fence we usually entered and left the depot through was only fifteen metres ahead, but to get to it we had to cross an empty stretch of car park. If anyone was nearby, they couldn't fail to spot us.

'It's safe,' Ameena whispered. 'Let's go.'

We scurried, doubled over, towards the fence, eyes searching the darkness for any sign of movement. The driver was no longer calling for help. I guessed that meant Barney – whoever he was – had turned up.

Without the shouting, and with no traffic on the road beyond the fence, there was only the soft sound of our feet on the tarmac to disturb the eerie silence.

But no. That wasn't quite true. There was another sound too. A rapid clicking, far away, but getting closer. Ameena heard it at the same time I did. She straightened up, mid-run, and looked behind us. Even in the dark, I saw her face go pale.

I glanced back in the direction of the clicking. Dave the driver stood over by one of the coaches, watching us. He was talking into a mobile phone, probably calling the police, but that, right now, wasn't the problem.

The problem was about halfway between him and us. The problem was a large brown-and-black dog. And the problem was racing across the depot, its paws clicking against the road with every bound.

'Get 'em, Barney!' Dave cried, taking the phone away from his ear for just a moment.

Ameena and I doubled our speed as Barney the Rottweiler opened his jaws and let rip with a frenzy of angry barking.

'Hurry!' Ameena cried, before realising I was already in the process of overtaking her. We hit the fence mid-sprint, slamming into the chain-link metal and making the whole thing shake. Down at our feet, the hole was only big enough to take one of us at a time. Behind us, Barney's barking rose to fever pitch.

Ameena glanced upwards at the fence, which stood about three metres high. She flexed her fingers, reached up as high as she could, and began to climb.

'Go under, I'll go over,' she said. 'Move!'

The clicking and the barking were almost on me as I dropped to my knees and pushed at the broken chain-link. It folded outwards, then snagged on the grass verge on the other side.

'Get him, Barn!'

'Move!' Ameena cried. 'Move, move, move!'

I shoved harder and the bottom of the fence pinged free. The ground froze my belly as I dropped down and wriggled my way through. I barely noticed it, or the scratching of the metal fence down the whole length of my back.

The teeth, though, I did notice. They were hard to miss. They bit into my jeans, just above my ankle. I felt the dog's hot breath against my skin, heard it growl deep down at the back of its throat.

'Good boy, Barney!' the driver called over. 'Good boy. Keep a hold of him, now.'

Ameena dropped on to the grass just a few centimetres from my head. I tried to kick the dog away, but my legs were pinned between the fence and the ground. I felt Ameena's hands around my own as, just a few streets away, a siren began to scream.

'Cops,' Ameena groaned. She pulled hard on my arms, almost popping them from their sockets. 'Come on!'

'I'm trying!' I told her. I twisted and the dog lost his grip. Ameena managed to drag me forwards a few more centimetres before those jaws were at my leg again. I hissed in pain as the teeth scraped against my ankle bone. An all-too-familiar tingle buzzed through my head.

'N-no!' I gasped, but I was too late to stop it. Fuelled by my fear, my abilities took control. I heard Barney yelp as an invisible wind sent him bouncing backwards across the tarmac.

Ameena pulled harder, dragging me through the fence

and up on to the strip of grass that ran alongside the pavement.

'Don't want to use your powers, eh?' she asked, breathing heavily.

'Didn't do it on purpose,' I wheezed, checking the back of my leg for damage but finding no real harm done.

'You *so* could have made us that cake,' she muttered. She looked along the street, to where we could hear the police car drawing ever closer. 'You know,' she said, zipping up her jacket and marching quickly away from the approaching siren, 'maybe heading for your place isn't such a bad idea after all.'

I'd expected the journey home to be a long, difficult one with lots of walking and hitch-hiking involved. It turned out I was wrong.

Ameena had produced some more money she'd just "found" lying around, and we'd taken the bus most of the way. It was the same bus company whose depot we'd only just escaped from that morning. Fortunately, it wasn't the same driver. This one barely gave us a second glance when we got on at the station, even though we must've looked a right state.

We dozed most of the way, the shuddering and shaking of the seats beneath us rocking our exhausted bodies to sleep within minutes of the engine starting.

It was the driver who woke us up, nudging us to let us know we'd reached our stop. I sat upright and looked out of the window, blinking away the sleep and trying to figure out where we were. It didn't look familiar, and I was about to let the driver know this wasn't our stop when I remembered we'd decided to get off at the next town over, rather than at my village itself. If the police were still looking for us – and they would be – stepping off the bus right outside my house probably wouldn't be a very wise move.

And so, we'd hopped off the coach and taken the long way round to my village, walking through woodland and long grass, keeping as far away from the road as possible. It was slow going, and – thanks to my frequent need to rest – took us almost as long as the bus journey.

Which is why it was getting dark again by the time

we reached our destination. Not home. Not quite. Not yet. We made instead for the old abandoned house just across from mine. The house where my childhood imaginary friend, Mr Mumbles, had almost killed me. Twice.

The Keller House.

It was the same height as all the other houses on the street, but it seemed impossibly tall, like a tower or castle stretching up into the cloudy night sky. I stood on the pavement, looking in. There was the garden Mumbles had chased me across. There was the pool house, where I'd almost drowned. And up there, the roof, where both Ameena and I had almost died of cold.

'You OK?' Ameena's voice came at me from nowhere, snapping me back to the present.

'Fine,' I said, trying to smile but forgetting how. I clambered over the fence. We were round the back of the house, well out of sight, but I still felt too exposed. 'Come on, someone will see us here.'

The grass crunched beneath our feet, brittle with frost.

The last time I'd been in this garden it had been slick with mud. I'd struggled to keep my footing as I ran from Mr Mumbles. Even now, I had an overwhelming urge to look behind me. I half-expected to see him there, striding slowly across the lawn, his eyes glaring hatred at me.

He wasn't there, of course. He was in the Darkest Corners, the hell-like alternate dimension where all imaginary friends go after they're cast aside. And besides, he wasn't after me any more. He'd saved my life when I'd been trapped in the Darkest Corners. He'd promised to look after I.C., the little kid I'd met over there. He'd changed. In some weird way, I suppose we were... no, not friends. Allies, maybe. Or no longer enemies, at least.

But none of that made the Keller House seem less frightening. I'd been terrified of it long before Mr Mumbles had come back, and I was still terrified of it now. But it was empty and it had a roof and it was close to home. Much as I hated to admit it, it was the perfect place to hide while we kept an eye on my house.

The front door was boarded shut, and had been for as long as I could remember. But the nails were rusty and the wood was weak and it only took two or three sharp tugs from Ameena to create us an opening.

'Ladies first,' she said, gesturing for me to go inside.

'No, after you,' I replied, and I really hoped she wouldn't argue.

'Chicken,' she smirked. I took hold of the wooden board and pulled it back as she squeezed inside. 'Whoa, it stinks,' she coughed. 'Looks OK, though. Come on through.'

Ameena braced her hands against the wood from the inside. I released my grip, screwed my courage up to a ball in the centre of my stomach, and inched my way into the house.

The smell raced to meet me as I crawled inside. It was the smell of the attic in my house – damp and stale – but ten times worse. I zipped the top of my jacket over my mouth and nose and straightened up. My hands felt sticky or wet – I couldn't really tell which – from crawling on the carpet. I wiped them on my thighs, suddenly revolted at the thought of what I might have been touching.

Because I couldn't see what was on the carpet. Nor, for that matter, could I see the carpet itself. Outside had been dark, but in the house, with the board back in place, the total absence of light left us blind.

I tried to speak, but my throat had gone dry. It was no surprise, really. For years I'd lived in fear of the Keller House, and now here I was, standing inside it in complete blackness. What made it worse was that when I was young I wasn't all that sure if monsters were real. Now I knew they were. And most of them wanted me dead.

Something brushed against my back and I screamed – a high, shrill scream, with all the manliness of a three-year-old girl.

'Easy kiddo,' Ameena snorted. 'Just me.'

'Don't do that!' I gasped. 'I could've... really hurt you.'

'Yeah, in your dreams, maybe,' she said. 'Now follow me, I think I can see light.'

'How am I supposed to follow you? I can't see a thing.'

I felt her grab and fumble at my sleeve, then her hand slipped into mine. Her palm felt warm against my cold skin as our fingers interlocked. 'That better?' she asked.

I nodded, unable to speak again, but for different reasons. She couldn't have seen my nod, but she took my silence as a "yes".

'Right, this way,' she said, and I found myself dragged, unresisting, further into the room.

At first, I still couldn't see anything, but as she led me across the floor, I began to make out little dents in the darkness. The outline of an armchair. The edge of a low-hanging ceiling light. A corner of a picture on the wall. It was enough to give the impression that Mr Keller, the house's former owner, had just gone out one morning and never returned. In fact, that's exactly what he had done, but I'd assumed the house would have been cleared out at some point since then. I'd assumed wrong.

Ameena stopped. Her warmth left my hand as she released her grip. Just ahead of us, a door creaked slowly open at her push, letting a dim orange glow seep through. A narrow staircase stood before us. The carpet that covered the stairs was tatty and threadbare. Floral-patterned wallpaper peeled in long sheets from the walls on either side.

The upstairs landing was bathed in the same orange light as the stairs. It was faint and watery, only barely lifting the blanket of shadow, but it was better than the darkness we'd just left.

'Someone left a lamp on, you think?' Ameena asked. She chewed on the knuckle of one of the fingers on her left hand. I couldn't remember ever seeing her so nervous.

'You should know,' I said. 'Was there a light on when you stayed here?'

She looked at me blankly for a moment, her eyebrows dipping into the beginning of a frown. It passed as quickly as it had come, and she gave a casual shrug. 'Didn't notice,' she said. 'But then I didn't exactly hang around long.'

That surprised me. As far as I'd known, Ameena had been sleeping rough in the Keller House for almost two weeks after our encounter with Mr Mumbles. I wanted to ask her where she'd gone instead, but there was no time for questions.

With a final glance back at me, Ameena took hold of the old wooden banister, and crept cautiously up the stairs.

Chapter Three

THE STAKEOUT

Dust swirled up from the carpet with every step we took. It danced in the air like a swarm of tiny agitated insects. I was sticking as close to Ameena as I could. For maybe the first time ever, she was taking her time, testing each step before putting her full weight on it, in case it should crumble beneath her.

Upstairs the same threadbare carpet covered the floor and the same peeling wallpaper drooped from the walls. A bare bulb hung from the ceiling, thick with dust and cobwebs. The bulb wasn't the source of the light, though. That seeped in through a door at the far end of the landing. It was one of four doors, and the only one standing open.

Unfortunately, it wasn't open far enough for us to see inside the room.

The smell of damp was worse up here. It reached down my throat, making me gag. Ameena seemed unaffected as she crossed the landing, making for the half-open door.

She stopped when she reached it, moved to push it the rest of the way open, then hesitated. For a long time, she didn't look as if she was going to make any further movement.

'Want me to go first?' I asked, adding *please say no, please say no, please say no* in my head.

'No.'

'*Thank God!*'

She shot me a scowl.

'Sorry,' I mumbled. 'Didn't mean to say that out loud.'

With a shake of her head, Ameena put her palm against the door and gave it a nudge. It swung open a little, then caught on the carpet, forcing her to step closer and give it another shove. It opened with a low, ominous creak.

The glow of a streetlight shone in through the bedroom window, and I remembered that none of the upstairs windows had ever been boarded up. I'd lain awake in bed countless times when I was younger, convinced I'd seen shadows moving within the bedrooms of the Keller House while I was closing my own curtains.

And now, here I was, my own shadow moving across the mould-stained wallpaper, and through the window, across the garden – my house. My bedroom. My curtains. I stared into my darkened room, wishing I could transport myself back to one of those nights, lying in bed, Mum assuring me the Keller House was empty.

I hoped she was right.

'Hey, check it out!' Ameena's voice broke the spell and I turned from the window. She was sitting propped up on a single bed, her muddy boots leaving marks on the yellowing covers, her back resting against the padded headboard. 'Bagsy the bed.'

'You can have it,' I said, queasy at the thought. 'There could be anything crawling about in there. I'll sleep on the floor.'

'Oh, like that's better?'

I looked down and winced. The carpet was a mess of mould and mouse droppings. Mushrooms sprouted from the soggier patches, all of them different shapes and sizes, all of them probably deadly.

A fat black insect with a shiny back scuttled past my foot. I watched it scurry across the carpet, through a clump of the mushrooms, and into a dark hole in the skirting board.

'We should check out the other rooms,' I said, fighting the urge to scratch my skin until it bled. 'They might be less...'

'Revolting?'

I nodded. 'Hopefully.'

'Right then,' Ameena said, swinging her legs off the bed and taking a kick at the closest mushroom crop. 'Lead the way, kiddo.'

* * *

Of the three remaining upstairs rooms, one was another equally filthy bedroom, one was a small box room with nothing in it, and the last was a bathroom so horrific we both agreed never to speak of it again.

The box room was where we settled in the end. It was completely bare – exposed wooden floorboard, unpainted plasterboard walls – and, as a result, hadn't decayed as badly as the other rooms. It also looked straight on to the side of my house, meaning we could see if anyone came or went through the front door or the back. The perfect place for a stakeout.

I stood at the window, looking across the gardens to my house. In the past twenty minutes I'd seen just one car pass along the street. I'd ducked as soon as I spotted the headlights, but the car didn't slow down as it continued along the road and turned the corner at the far end.

'Anything?' Ameena asked from right behind me. I hadn't even heard her approach.

I shook my head. 'No. Looks deserted.'

'We expected that,' she said, as tactfully as she could. 'I'm sure she's fine. Your mum. There'd have been something in the papers if she'd... if her condition had changed.'

'I know,' I replied, still not taking my eyes off the house. 'I want to go over.'

Without looking, I could guess at Ameena's expression. 'That'd just be stupid,' she said. 'You'd get caught.'

'Who by?' I asked, gesturing across to the house. To my home. 'There's no one there.'

'They're bound to be watching, though. Think about it.'

'I won't be long,' I told her. 'I just want to see it. Maybe get some clean clothes.'

I stepped back from the window, still not looking at her. She caught me by the shoulder. I stopped, but didn't turn. 'Don't do it,' she said. 'You can't help anyone if you're locked up.'

'I'm not helping anyone now,' I said, shrugging myself free. 'I won't be long. There's no one coming.'

Halfway to the door, I stopped, as a blue light lit up the room. It faded quickly, then brightened again. The pattern repeated, over and over, and I knew what was happening even before Ameena spoke.

'Cops,' she said, matter-of-factly.

I crossed to the window. 'Here?'

'At yours.'

Ameena stood to one side of the window frame, leaning out just a little to watch what was happening below. I took the opposite side and peeped out.

A single police car stood outside my front garden, its blue light flashing, its headlamps blazing.

'No one coming, eh?' Ameena said. I didn't meet her gaze.

'What's it doing?' I asked, my voice a whisper, as if whoever was in the police car might hear me.

Before Ameena answered, the driver's door opened and a woman in a police uniform stepped out. From here she looked young – mid-twenties, maybe – but it was hard to tell for sure.

She glanced along the street and up at my house. I pulled back, expecting her to look our way, but she didn't.

Instead she walked around to the other side of the car and opened the rear door. I almost cried out as a familiar head of grey hair bobbed up into view.

'Nan!' I said, wishing I could bang on the glass, wishing I could run to her. 'It's my nan!'

Ameena didn't reply. I tore my eyes away from Nan long enough to see the worry on Ameena's face. Only then did the first stirrings of panic begin.

'Why's Nan here?' I wondered aloud. 'Why would they bring her to the house?'

'Maybe she's picking something up for your mum.'

'At this time of night?'

'Maybe it's something she really needs.'

'But why send Nan? She doesn't know where things are. She can barely think straight these days.' It was true. Dementia had been devouring Nan's memories for years now. Sometimes she didn't recognise any of us, herself included.

'Maybe...' Ameena began, but nothing followed it. She was all out of maybes.

The policewoman let Nan take her arm. I watched them shuffle slowly up the path. It was the policewoman who unlocked the door. I kept watching until they both disappeared inside.

'What if something's happened to Mum?' I asked, feeling the panic rise up into my throat. 'What if they've come to sort out all her stuff? What if she's...'

'They've left the lights going,' Ameena said, cutting me short. I looked down at the car. Sure enough, the blue light was still flashing and the beams of the headlamps still cut through the gloom. 'They can't plan on staying long.'

'Why's it flashing?' I asked. 'I thought that was just for emergencies.'

Ameena shrugged. 'Don't ask me.'

We didn't speak again for a while, just watched for Nan and the policewoman emerging. Eventually, we got tired of standing and sat on the floor, taking it in turns to raise up on to our knees and look over at the house. Lights had come on in all the rooms, but other than that, there had been nothing to report.

'How long's that been?' I asked.

'About an hour,' Ameena said. 'Give or take ten minutes.'

I looked at the car, its lights still burning. 'Her battery's going to go flat if she doesn't get a move on.'

Ameena yawned. 'Mine too.' She lay down on her side, propping her head up on her hand. 'Think I'm going to get some rest. You should too.'

'I'm fine,' I said, forcing my heavy eyelids open to prove my point. 'I'm going to keep watching.'

'Wake me up if anything happens,' she answered, rolling on to her back and interlocking her fingers behind her head. 'Hey, cool,' she said, looking past me, up towards the cloudy night sky. 'It's snowing.'

I raised my eyes in time to see a tiny white dot drift by on the other side of the glass. Another fell a moment later, then another, and another. In just a few minutes, the sky was filled with a hundred thousand falling flakes.

'It's heavy too,' I said, but Ameena's only reply was a

soft snore. 'No stamina,' I muttered, then I yawned, rested my chin on the windowsill, and settled in for a long, lonely stakeout.

I woke up with my forehead against the cold glass and soft January sunlight in my eyes. Several centimetres of snow were piled up on the window ledge, so white it was almost glowing.

'Crap!' I cursed. I tried to stand up but my legs were numb from being folded beneath me and I quickly fell back down again.

'What? What's wrong?' Ameena asked, wide awake and on her feet before she'd finished speaking.

'I fell asleep,' I explained, furious with myself. 'I missed them coming out!'

'Um... no you didn't.'

I looked down at the front of my house. The police car was still there. Its headlamps were dim and the blue light had been covered by the snow that continued to fall. The car hadn't moved all night.

'That's weird,' I said. I looked to Ameena for reassurance. 'That's weird, right?'

She nodded. 'That is definitely weird.'

The lights were still on in the house. I studied all the windows in turn, trying to make out any movement within them. Nothing. As far as I could see, the house was completely still.

'Why would they still be there?' I asked, not really expecting an answer. 'It's been hours. They should've come out long before now.'

'Kyle.' Ameena spoke the word quietly, but I couldn't miss the tremble in her voice.

'What?'

She didn't reply, just nodded towards the back garden. Towards the streaks of dark red that coloured the snow.

I was out of the room in a heartbeat, bounding down into the darkness at the bottom of the stairs. The electricity tingled across my scalp, and this time I didn't resist. I imagined the board being torn from the front door, pictured the wood and the rusty nails being yanked sharply away.

The board gave a *crack* and fell outwards as I approached and a dim, watery light seeped in. I hurried outside and found myself stumbling, knee-deep, through snow. I hesitated, just for a moment, wondering how this much of the stuff could possibly have fallen in one night, but then I was running again, heading for the fence, no longer worried about being seen.

Ameena crunched along behind me, struggling to keep up. The snow slowed me down, but I reached the fence in no time and vaulted over it.

I plopped down into the marshmallow whiteness of my garden, staggered forwards, then set off running again, making for the back door. The snow was falling heavily, making it hard to see more than a few metres in any direction. I was running through the red streaks almost before I saw them. Their slick wetness sparkled atop the snow, slowly taking on a pinkish hue as more flakes fell.

I looked up, blinking against the blizzard, and saw the back door stood ajar. Not bothering to wait for Ameena, I crunched up the stone steps, through the open door, and into a blood-soaked warzone that had once been my kitchen.

Chapter Four

COP OUT

'**N**an? *Nan?*'

I raced through the kitchen, past the upturned table and the broken chairs, past the blood-spattered cabinets and the shattered glass.

'Good grief!' Ameena muttered, appearing at the back door just as I charged through into the living room.

'Nan, where are you?' I called. My voice was absorbed by the silence of the house. The living room was a mess, but not in the same league as the kitchen. The coffee table was in pieces and the TV was face down on the carpet, but there was no blood. No Nan, either.

I made for the stairs, then pulled myself together enough to collect one of the legs of the broken coffee table. It was a short piece of wood – about forty-five centimetres from top to bottom – but it was thick and it was heavy and I'd be able to do some damage with it if I had to.

'Any sign of her?' Ameena asked, joining me at the bottom of the stairs. She'd had the same idea as me, and now carried a knife she'd lifted from the wooden block in the kitchen. She held it with the blade flat against her wrist, half-concealed, but ready to strike.

'Not yet,' I said. I called up the stairs. 'Nan? Nan, are you up there?'

A groan. A whimper. Faint, but there. I was halfway up the stairs when I heard it again, three-quarters of the way before I realised it had come from the living room.

I turned, bounded back down half a dozen steps, and that's when I realised I had been wrong. There *was* blood in the living room. So much blood.

It started on the wall just by the kitchen door, a metre and a half off the ground, and streaked straight upwards – a thick smear of it in one continuous line across the ceiling.

The trail stopped almost exactly above the couch. The

whimper came again and I took the last of the stairs in a single leap. Ameena was already pulling the couch aside. I saw the police uniform before I was halfway there.

She lay on her back, her hands on her belly, one eye wide open, one battered shut. Blood pumped through her fingers, ran down her arms, seeped into the carpet, *drip, drip, drip*. Half of her face was a swollen mess of purple and black. Her one open eye stared upwards, but not at the ceiling, at something beyond the ceiling that only she could see.

Her breathing came in shallow gasps, two or three a second, in-out, in-out, in-out.

'What do we do?' Ameena asked.

'Call an ambulance.'

'What? But... they'll bring more cops. You'll get—'

'Call an ambulance!' I shouted. 'She's dying!'

There was a moment's hesitation, and for just a fraction of a second I thought she was going to refuse. But then she was clambering over the couch, reaching for the sideboard, picking up the phone.

I knelt down by the policewoman, wishing I knew how to help her. Her eye was bulging, the pupil fully dilated so there was no colour left, just a circle of black. I had been right last night – she was young. Late twenties at the most.

'It's dead.'

I looked up. Ameena was standing over us, the phone in her hand. 'No dial tone. Weather, maybe?'

Maybe.

Maybe not.

I touched one of the policewoman's hands, meaning to move it aside so I could see how badly she was hurt – as if the pints of blood painting the inside of the house weren't enough of a clue.

The moment my fingers touched hers, though, she grabbed my hand and squeezed it tight, clinging to it as if it was the only thing anchoring her to life. I didn't pull away, just held on to her and let her hold on to me. I wanted to ask her what had happened and where Nan was, but I knew I'd get no answer.

Instead I said the only thing I could think of. A lie. 'It's OK. You're going to be OK.'

I watched a single tear form in her open eye. It trickled sideways, meandering across her temple and over her ear. By the time it dripped on to the carpet, her hand no longer gripped on to mine. I carefully rested it back on her stomach, closed over her eye, and stood up.

'Someone else dead,' I said, after a long silence, 'because of me.'

I hated the matter-of-fact tone of my voice. Hated the fact I wasn't shaking or crying or screaming about the woman's death. The cold fact of it was, I'd seen worse.

'You don't know that, kiddo.'

But we both knew I was right.

It was happening again. Someone – or something – had come looking for me, and another innocent person had found themselves caught in the crossfire.

I took hold of the table leg again, tightening my grip until my knuckles shone white. I set my jaw, clenching my teeth together. Someone else dead. Because of me.

The stairs passed in a haze. I was at the top before I realised I'd moved. The lights were on up here, all four doors open. I looked in my bedroom, in my wardrobe, under my bed. Nothing there, so I moved on, no longer interested in a trip down Memory Lane. I needed to find Nan and I wanted to find whoever had killed the policewoman. Nothing else mattered.

Nan's old room, empty. Bathroom, empty. No damage to either and no blood stains on the walls. I turned to the last door and that's when I did hesitate, taking a second to compose myself before stepping inside Mum's bedroom.

Her bed was unmade. It must've been that way since the morning she'd sent me to stay with Marion. The morning she'd been attacked by the Crowmaster, beaten so badly she was still in a coma. And all because of me.

Her dressing gown lay across the duvet. She'd worn it when she'd talked to me about going away – an all-night conversation in which I'd done nothing but whinge and complain. If she didn't pull through, that would be the last proper talk we ever had. I pushed the thought from my mind. She'd pull through. She had to.

'Any sign?'

I turned to find Ameena in the upstairs hallway, knife held ready. 'Nothing,' I said, and she lowered the blade to her side. 'No one's here.'

'Great,' she said, sighing. 'What now?'

'We go outside,' I said. 'We look for her. We find her. We've got to find her.'

Ameena's hand was on my shoulder. 'We will. She'll be OK.'

OK. Like the policewoman was OK.

'But we'd better wrap up,' Ameena continued. 'Or we'll freeze in that snow.'

'We'll grab coats from the cupboard downstairs,' I said, turning from Mum's room and striding along the landing. 'There should be one about your—'

THUD.

The sound came from the living room. It was a single low knock; the sound of something heavy hitting something solid.

Ameena had the knife raised in an instant, the other hand on my chest, holding me behind her. But I was beyond that now. For too long I'd relied on Ameena to protect me, when really it should've been the other way round.

I pushed her hand aside, more forcefully than I meant to, and crossed to the stairs. I may have been desperate to find Nan, but I wasn't stupid, and didn't rush straight down to the living room. After creeping down a couple of the stairs, I squatted down and looked through the gaps in the wooden banister.

Nothing moved in the room below. I tiptoed further down, feeling Ameena close behind me.

I should've been watching out for trouble, but as I reached the bottom of the stairs my eyes were fixed on only one spot. A patch of carpet, stained with blood. A patch that should've been covered by the policewoman's body.

'Where'd she go?' I muttered, finally looking around. The living room appeared to be exactly as we'd left it, minus one fresh corpse.

'Maybe she got better,' Ameena suggested.

'What, better than "dead"?'

'Well, you can't exactly get much worse.'

I stepped further into the room, ready to swing with the table leg. 'Someone took her,' I said. 'Someone came in and took her.'

There was silence in the living room then, broken finally by Ameena asking the question that was bothering us both.

'Why would someone do that?'

'I don't know.'

'And *who* would do it?'

'Whoever killed her,' I said.

'Nah. They'd have just taken her at the time, surely?'

I dug my fingernails into my palms. 'Not if they were already carrying somebody else.'

It took a moment for what I was saying to sink in, then: 'Oh.'

Nan. Had whoever took the policewoman's body already taken Nan? Just the idea of it made my heart race and my legs spring into action. I ran through to the ruined kitchen and hurled myself through the back door, out into the swirling snowstorm.

'Nan!' I shouted, but the falling flakes seemed to absorb most of the sound. I staggered along the path and out through the open back gate, wading knee-deep through snow that was now only faintly tinged with pink. 'Nan, *where are you?*'

'Kyle, come back!' Ameena's shout was a whisper in the distance. I blundered on, along the back of my row of houses, shouting for Nan the whole way.

The cold gripped my legs up to the knees as I forced my way on. My hands were raised in front of me, shielding my eyes from the driving snow. My village gets its fair share of snow in the winter, but this was like nothing I'd ever seen before. It was too severe, too sudden to be natural. Something had to be causing it. *Great.* Another thing for me to worry about. Always one more thing.

I emerged from behind the houses into the street. The snow covered the few cars here like a thick white fur. Normally I'd be able to see my front garden, but the blizzard made it impossible to see more than a few metres in any direction.

The houses around me were in darkness, but the streetlights were on. For all the difference they made. It might have been early morning, but barely a glimmer of sunlight was making it through the snowstorm. I stood in the pool of light cast by one of the street lamps, making myself as visible as I could.

'Nan!' I cried. 'I'm here! Where are you?'

A hand caught me roughly by the shoulder and spun me around. I found myself looking into Ameena's scowling face. 'What the hell do you think you're doing?' she demanded.

'I was—'

'Being an idiot?'

'No! I was—'

'On a suicide mission?'

'What? No!'

'Well, what then?' she snapped. 'Because, from what I can see, you're freezing to death, standing in plain sight and making a racket that's going to draw the attention of everyone in town.' She stepped out of the pool of light, dragging me with her. 'Not to mention the attention of whatever killed that cop.'

'I have to find Nan,' I told her.

'I know. But here's a suggestion – don't get violently killed before you do. Stealth, kiddo. Stealth.'

I thought about the policewoman, and about the blood on the ceiling and walls. 'OK,' I said quietly. 'Point made.'

'Good,' she said, giving me a gentle punch on the shoulder. 'Now, come on, let's go get warmed up then we'll figure out what to do.' She began trudging up the street towards my front garden, glancing at the houses on either side of the road as we walked. 'It's just a miracle no one heard you and came out to see what the ruckus was about.'

'Yeah,' I said, only half-listening. 'A miracle.'

'Didn't even see a light come on,' she continued. 'Must all be deaf, the noise you were making.'

'Deaf,' I agreed, trudging along behind her. 'Yeah.'

I stopped walking.

'Wait,' I said.

'What?'

I looked across at the other side of the street, where I could just make out the darkened outlines of six houses.

'Why've we stopped?' Ameena was asking. I didn't answer.

The houses on this side of the street were in darkness too. Now that we were closer, I could make out the lights we'd left on in my house, but they were the only ones on in the entire block.

There were a few vehicles parked along the street – a couple of cars, the van of the window-cleaner who lived at number five – but nothing moved in any direction along the road.

'Listen,' I said.

A pause, then, 'Listen to what?'

'To nothing,' I said.

Another pause, then, 'Are you winding me up? What you on about?'

'It's quiet,' I whispered. 'There's not a sound.'

She listened, properly this time, without speaking.

'It's early,' she said, offering an explanation.

'Not that early. People should be up and about.' I nodded across the street. 'They should at least have their lights on.'

Ameena looked at each house in turn, considering this. Then she scooped up some snow, squashed it into a ball shape, and launched it at the closest bedroom window.

Her aim was spot on. The snowball hit the glass with a loud *thonk*, and I had to resist the urge to run away and hide. We stood watching the window, waiting for a light to come on.

'Try another one,' she said, when it became clear the room was staying dark. 'Try them all.'

We worked quickly, making snowballs, chucking them at windows. Most of mine found their target. All of Ameena's found theirs. We hit over twenty windows. No one appeared at any of them.

'Empty,' I said, voicing what we'd both already guessed. 'They're all empty.'

'Or maybe...'

I turned to Ameena. 'Maybe what?'

'Maybe the people inside just can't come to the window.'

I looked to the closest house, shrouded in darkness like all the others. A shiver ran the length of my spine, nothing to do with the cold.

'Only one way to find out,' I said.

The gate *squeaked* as I pushed it open and slowly, quietly, we approached the front door.

Chapter Five

TOES IN THE SUGAR

'It's open.'

Ameena drew her breath in sharply through her teeth. 'That doesn't bode well.'

I gave the door a gentle push and it swung inwards, revealing a shadowy hallway. A brass number 9 was screwed on to the front of the door. Number 9 was Mrs Angelo's house. I couldn't tell you much about Mrs Angelo, other than that she was in her sixties, and always used to give out the best sweets at Halloween. Not much of a biography, really.

I tried to call Mrs Angelo's name, but my throat had tightened so the sound that came out was little more than a whisper. I coughed and tried again. 'Mrs Angelo? Are you there?'

Ameena pushed past me and strode into the hallway. 'Helloooo?' she shouted at the top of her voice. 'Anyone home?'

'What happened to stealth?' I asked.

She shrugged. 'Stealth got boring. Shut the door.'

I hesitated, unsure, but then quietly clicked the door closed. Ameena flicked a switch and the hallway was bathed in light. I realised for the first time that my hands were blue with cold. Jamming them under my armpits, I followed Ameena into the living room.

A tattered armchair and a saggy old couch sat empty in the room. The TV was off. An old grandfather clock tick-tocked solemnly in the corner.

'Not in there,' Ameena said, and we both backed out into the hall. I tried the kitchen next. The door was ajar, and swung open at a prod from my foot.

The room was empty, but the fridge door hung open,

casting a pale yellow glow across the rest of the kitchen. A mug of tea stood on the worktop beside the fridge.

'Cold,' Ameena said, touching the side of the mug. 'Guess she changed her mind about having a cuppa.'

'Or something changed it for her.'

'I wasn't going to mention that,' she said. 'In case, you know... you wet yourself or something.'

'Funny,' I sighed. 'Come on, she might be upstairs.'

Something *crunched* softly beneath Ameena's foot. We both looked down to find a bag of sugar on the floor, its contents spilled across the lino. Our attention was instantly drawn to the shape that was clearly visible in the scattered granules. We studied it for a long, long time.

'What the hell made that?' Ameena asked, at last.

'Dunno,' I replied.

'Well, if you *are* going to wet yourself, now might be the perfect time.'

I stared down at the shape in the sugar. A shape that could only be described as an enormous, three-toed footprint. 'You know,' I whispered, 'I might just take you up on that.'

'Should we search the rest of the house?' Ameena asked. She didn't take her eyes from the print. It was about forty centimetres in length, and the same again at its widest point, up near the three saucer-sized toeprints.

'Probably,' I said, though I doubt I sounded convinced.

'Thought you'd say that.' Ameena gave a grim nod, then swept the sugar aside with her foot. 'Come on, then,' she said. 'Let's get it over with.'

Mrs Angelo's house was laid out differently to mine, even though they were on the same block. The stairs in my house led up from the living room, but in Mrs Angelo's they started in the hall. Two steps, then a sharp left turn and more stairs leading to the upper floor.

The stairway was narrow, but neither of us felt like pushing ahead. Flicking on the light, we made our way up, shoulder to shoulder, side by side. Each step brought a groan of protest from the floorboard beneath us. If anything was up there, it would already know we were coming.

'Anyone home?' The sound of Ameena's voice in the cramped space made me jump.

'*Sssssh!*' I hissed.

'Why?'

'Um, well, *giant footprint*,' I whispered. 'Remember?'

'Um, well, *narrow staircase*,' she said.

'So?'

She gave a sigh, then spoke slowly, as if explaining to a child. 'Big thing no fit up small stairs.'

I thought about this for a moment. The footprint we saw suggested an enormous creature. Rhino-sized, maybe bigger. A rhino couldn't fit up these stairs in a million years. Not even with someone pushing it really hard from behind.

'Anyway, we don't even know if it was a footprint,' she said.

'Oh, it was,' I nodded. 'It was definitely a footprint.'

We were almost at the top of the stairs now and began to creep even more slowly. 'How do you know?'

'Because I don't want it to be a footprint,' I said. 'Because the *worst possible thing* it could be is the scary big footprint of something that wants to kill us. And the worst possible things keep happening to me lately.' I took a deep breath, stopping my rant before it became too loud. 'I know it's a footprint, because with my recent luck, it couldn't be anything else.'

She shrugged. 'Fair point. But it still couldn't fit up the stairs.'

We stepped on to an upper landing awash with the smells of old lady. Talcum powder. Lavender. Something that could've been cabbage. As I breathed them in, my memories of Mrs Angelo became pin-sharp in my mind. I remembered my last meeting with her, chatting to her for a few seconds on Christmas Eve as I'd delivered her card.

Mum was always late writing Christmas cards, but even for her, 10 p.m. on Christmas Eve was cutting it fine. I'd planned to drop the card through the letterbox and move on, but Mrs Angelo had clocked me coming up the path and had come to the door to talk to me.

She was the last person I'd seen before Christmas Day. Before Mumbles. Before any of this had started. Mrs Angelo – and her smell – were normality. They represented the last moments of my old life, a life where the only things I had to worry about were my mum's cooking and a regular hammering from school bully, Billy Gibb. A life I'd go back to in a heartbeat.

'Ssssh!'

I blinked, Ameena's hissing in my ear dragging me back to the present. 'I didn't say anything,' I whispered.

'Ssssh! Shut up. Listen,' she said, clamping her hand over my mouth. 'Hear that?'

It was a complete role reversal from just a few moments ago, outside the house, when I'd been trying to draw Ameena's attention to the absolute silence of the street. But there *was* something to hear now. A slow, irregular *knock-knock-knock*, coming from the other side of the door at the end of the landing.

'Mrs Angelo?' I said.

Knock. Knock. Knock.

I crept closer, Ameena following behind, scanning for trouble. No voice answered from within the room. 'Mrs Angelo,' I said again. 'Is that you?'

Knock. Knock-knock-knock.

'Maybe it's Morse Code,' Ameena suggested.

'Do you know Morse Code?' I asked hopefully.

She snorted. 'Don't be ridiculous.'

'Right. Didn't think so.'

We were met by more knocking when we reached the door. It wasn't loud, little more than a tapping against the other side of the wood, really. It seemed to come from all over the door – a knock at the bottom, followed by something bumping against the middle, then again up near head-height.

There was another sound too, that I could only hear now we were closer. It was a shuffling, rubbing sound, as if something was brushing against the other side of the door between knocks.

'Hello?' I said, trying the handle. It turned and I eased the door open a crack, but a weight pressed against it from within the room, stopping it opening more than those few millimetres.

'Mrs Angelo? Are you OK?'

Knock. Swish. Knock. Knock. Swish.

I looked to Ameena. 'What do we do?'

'Out the road,' she said, stepping back. 'I'll boot it open.'

I moved to block her. 'You can't do that! It could be Mrs Angelo in there.'

'Exactly,' Ameena nodded. 'She might be hurt.'

'Well getting a door in the face isn't going to do her much good, is it?'

Ameena thought about this. I could see she knew I was right. She'd never admit it, of course. 'Well, what do we do then?' she scowled. 'Just walk away?'

Knock. Knock. Knock. Was it my imagination, or was the tapping getting louder?

'The window,' I said. 'We'll look in the window.'

'Hold it steady,' I hissed, my legs shaking as I inched up another rung of the metal ladder. It had taken a few minutes of fumbling, but we'd managed to get it unstrapped from the roof of the window-cleaner's van and around the back of Mrs Angelo's house.

There were no lights on at the rear of the house either and it had taken a bit more time to figure out which was the window of the room with the knocking.

'I *am* holding it steady, it's not moving.'

'It's wobbling like crazy!' I insisted.

'No, Kyle, that's just you,' Ameena sighed. 'You sure you don't want me to go?'

I shook my head and took another step higher. I was only ten or eleven rungs up, but the falling snow meant I could no longer see the ground. 'No,' I said aloud, realising

Ameena probably couldn't see me either. 'She doesn't know you. If she sees you at the window she might get a fright.'

'Whereas she won't if she sees your ugly mug suddenly popping up?'

'At least she knows who I am,' I said, ignoring the jibe. 'Now shut up and hold it steady.'

She muttered something below her breath. I decided to ignore that too. Heaving myself up another two icy-cold rungs, I at last reached the window. The curtains were open, which was possibly the first piece of good luck I'd had in weeks.

It was dark in the bedroom, with only the early-morning daylight to pierce the gloom. I looked over to the door, and to the old woman in the ankle-length nightie who stood in front of it, her back to me.

'See anything?' Ameena's voice was muffled by the snow.

'Yeah,' I said, even if I wasn't quite sure exactly *what* I was seeing. 'She's in there all right.'

'Is she OK?'

I shakily took one hand from the ladder, then the other, leaving myself balancing. Cupping my hands against the glass, I looked more closely at Mrs Angelo.

She was walking – well, more sort of shuffling slowly – on the spot, apparently unaware of the door blocking her path. Her feet bumped against it, then her knees, then her forehead. That explained the knocking sounds, at least.

'Is she OK?' Ameena asked again, louder this time.

'I... I think so. I think she's sleepwalking.'

I knew you weren't supposed to wake someone up when they were sleepwalking, but the window was shut tight, and I couldn't think of any other way to get to her. Keeping one hand cupped against the glass, I used the other to rap three times on the window.

Over by the door, Mrs Angelo stopped shuffling. Her body went rigid, no doubt startled by the sudden sound. She showed no sign of turning around, though, so I knocked again. 'Mrs Angelo,' I called. 'It's me, Kyle, from down the street.'

That did it. Her whole body turned at the same time, her bare feet shuffling her around on the carpet until she was facing me. Her long, greying hair, which was usually tied in a bun, hung limply on either side of her face. Her mouth drooped open, revealing her shrunken, toothless gums.

But it was when I saw her eyes that I realised she definitely was *not* OK. Each eye was completely black – no iris, no pupil, no white bit – just two slivers of absolute darkness in the middle of her face.

'Something's wrong,' I started to shout, but Mrs Angelo's sudden lunge forward made the words catch in my throat. She moved much faster than I expected, crossing the room in a heartbeat.

I was still pressed against the glass when her face hit the other side with a *thonk*. I gasped in fright. Instinctively, I leaned backwards away from her, then remembered there was nothing but empty space behind me.

Clawing at the air, I grabbed for the top of the ladder, even as Mrs Angelo ferociously slammed herself against the glass. My fingertips brushed the ridged metal of the top rung, but couldn't find a grip. The winds seemed to whip up around me, and I found myself toppling backwards from the ladder, falling silently through the twirling, swirling snow.

Chapter Six

COP KILLERS?

The snow was a cushion of cold. I sank into it, stunned but unhurt by the fall. Flailing, I pulled myself into a sitting position and found Ameena standing over me, staring down.

'Do not even *think* about blaming that on me,' she said. She gave the ladder a shake. It didn't budge. 'Steady as a rock.'

I shook my head and pointed up. 'N-not the ladder,' I stammered, clambering to my feet.

'What, then?' Ameena asked, looking up to where the ladder vanished into a haze of white. 'What happened?'

'It's Mrs Angelo,' I said. 'It's Mrs Angelo, she's...

Something's...' I raised my hands to shoulder height and shrugged. 'Go look for yourself,' I said.

Ameena didn't hang around. Fixing her eyes on where the window would be, she stepped on to the ladder and began to climb. I watched her, fluttering my eyelids against the snow, until she was lost to the blizzard. There was silence then, before a steady *creaking* told me she was climbing back down.

With a soft *plop* she jumped the last few rungs and landed in a knee-deep snowdrift. She ran a hand through her long, dark hair, clearing away clumps of white that had begun to freeze there.

'I take it she's not normally like that?'

'What, foaming at the mouth and battering her face against the window?' I said. 'No. That's new.'

There was a loud, hollow-sounding *thonk* from the bedroom window. 'I'm not sure letting her out is such a good idea,' Ameena said.

I shook my head. 'What is g-going on?'

'You're freezing, that's what.' I saw Ameena take me

by the arm, but my skin was too numb to feel her touch. 'Let's get home and get changed.'

'But N-Nan...' I stammered. I realised that every time I opened my mouth, my lungs ached.

'We'll find her when you're warm,' Ameena said. She guided me ahead of her, still holding on to my arm. We both took a final look up in the direction of the window, before making our way back around the front of the house.

It was there that we saw her.

'Hey,' Ameena whispered, 'isn't that...?'

'The policewoman? I... I think so.'

She was standing along the road. We would never have seen her had she not been beneath the streetlight. Her neck was craned back so her face pointed to the sky. Her back was to us, but her arms hung limply by her sides so we could see the wash of blood over her hands.

'What's she up to?' I asked.

'Don't ask me. I thought she was dead,' Ameena

muttered. She took a step closer and raised her voice. 'Hey! I thought you were dead.'

The policewoman whipped around at the sound. Lit from behind, it was impossible to see her face, so we walked towards her, stooping low to shield our eyes from the snow.

We were halfway there when she moved. Her arms raised and her legs began to pump furiously, powering her through the snow in our direction. She opened her mouth and a sound – part scream, part roar, part... something else – emerged, shattering the near-silence.

'What's she—?' I began to ask, but she was on me before I could finish. She launched herself from three metres away, clearing the gap in one big bound. Her knees hit my chest, right below my chin. Fingers clawed at my face and pulled at my hair. I didn't feel myself falling until the snow came up to meet me.

'Get her off! Get her off!' I howled, my hands flailing as I fought to fend off the frenzied attack.

GRAAAAAAH! The sound started as a growl at the

back of her throat and quickly became a scream of animal rage. Her eyes, black as midnight, glared down at me as she thrashed and twisted and clawed.

CHOMP! Her teeth snapped shut just centimetres from my face. CHOMP! Again they clamped closed, close enough that I could feel the warmth of her breath. I dug my forearm in against her throat, trying to hold her back, but she was strong. Stronger than a dead woman had any right to be.

'What are you waiting for? Get her off!' I cried again.

'One sec,' Ameena replied.

'One sec? Are you mental? She's trying to – aaah, get off! She's trying to eat me!'

'Stop being such a cry-baby, she's not trying to—'

CHOMP!

'OK, she's trying to eat you.'

'I know! Do something about it!'

CLANG.

My extreme close-up of the policewoman's face vanished as a metal bucket was wedged violently down over her head.

'There,' Ameena said. 'She can't eat you now.'

With a shove, she sent the policewoman sprawling sideways on to the snow. I leapt up and we watched the woman for a moment, thrashing around, struggling to get back to her feet.

'You'd think she'd take the bucket off,' I said.

'I dunno, I shoved it on there pretty damn hard.'

'But she hasn't even tried pulling it off,' I pointed out. 'You'd think she'd at least give it a go.'

'I'm guessing she's not thinking straight,' Ameena replied. 'What with the growling and the black eyes and the biting and all that.'

'And the being dead,' I added quietly.

'Yeah. That can't help either.'

The policewoman didn't look frightening any more. Maybe it was the way she was slipping and sliding on her knees in the snow. Maybe it was the window-cleaner's bucket she had stuck on her head. Whatever, she looked more pathetic now than scary. I almost felt sorry for her.

'She's just like Mrs Angelo,' I said. 'That's what she was like at the bedroom window.' I looked over my shoulder to where Mrs Angelo's house stood, but all I could see was falling snow. 'Something's happening again, isn't it?'

Ameena nodded. 'Probably a safe bet.'

With a muffled scream of frustration, the policewoman tried once again to stand. Once again, she failed. Her legs moved in different directions and she fell backwards on to the snow. She kicked and punched the ground, like a toddler having a tantrum.

'What's wrong with her?'

'Dunno, but she definitely looks pale.' Ameena turned to me, grinning. '*Pale*. Get it? Pail. Because... the bucket. *Pale*.'

'Genius,' I sighed.

'Ah, you're just jealous you don't have my... Oh.'

Ameena's face fell. Down in the snow, the policewoman was sitting up. The bucket was not coming with her.

'It fell off,' I spluttered, stumbling backwards. The

policewoman's black eyes were darting between us, sizing us up. 'We need to run.'

Ameena raised her fists, bouncing cautiously on the balls of her feet. 'I can take her,' she said.

Squealing like an injured animal, the policewoman sprung forward on to all fours. Her face contorted and her lips pulled back until we could see every one of her teeth.

Ameena stopped bouncing. 'On second thoughts, let's go with your plan.'

She took off past me, running with her knees high to avoid tripping through the snow. I ran too, trying to follow in her footprints while keeping an eye on the policewoman.

'She's coming,' I yelled, as she began to give chase. She bounded along on all fours at first, then straightened up into a sprint. The snow barely slowed her down. She ploughed through it, gnashing and grabbing and howling at our backs.

'Move!' Ameena barked. 'Run faster.'

'I'm trying,' I protested. 'It's the snow, it—'

My foot snagged on a kerb and I landed face-first in a cushion of cold. I heard the policewoman screech in triumph.

'Kyle!'

Ameena's voice was far away. Too far.

That familiar electrical charge crackled across my scalp as I rolled on to my back. The policewoman was six metres away. Five. Four. Her teeth chomped the air. Her fingers curled into claws. She closed the remaining gap in three big bounds, too swiftly for me to do anything about it.

She was one step away from me when—

KA-RUNCH!

The car came from nowhere, slamming into her and sending her pinwheeling. She spun several times, before landing in an awkward and motionless heap on the ground.

With a squeal of brakes the car slid to a stop in the snow. Both front doors flew open. I couldn't see who got out of the driver's seat, but I recognised the passenger right away.

He was the boy who had made my school life hell for years. The boy who, just a few short weeks ago, had plunged a knife into my stomach. The boy who had created Caddie and Raggy Maggie, the psychotic imaginary girl and her equally deranged doll.

'Billy?' I gasped.

He looked down at me. If he was surprised, he didn't show it. 'It's you,' he said, matter-of-fact.

'Bullseye! I got her. Ooyah, check out the state of that,' cackled the boy on the other side of the car. He stepped around to the front and leaned one hand on the bonnet. In the other hand he gripped a short metal pole. Even though he was now standing in full view, I had no idea who he was.

'My cousin,' Billy said, as if reading my mind. 'Guggs.'

'*Guggs?*' Ameena snorted, jogging back to join us. 'Christ, that's unfortunate.'

'It's not my real name,' Guggs scowled. He had a fluffy, almost-but-not-quite moustache on his top lip and a neck that looked thicker than his head. Billy was big, but his cousin was bigger. '*Duh.*'

Ameena took my hand and pulled me up with one yank. 'So, what, you chose it yourself? Seriously? You called yourself Guggs?'

Guggs brought the arm holding the metal bar down to his side. He held it by his hip, sticking out, ready to swing. 'Got a problem with that?'

'You killed her,' I said, cutting the argument short. The policewoman was still an unmoving heap, her arms and legs twisted at unnatural angles, her face half-buried in the snow. 'You killed her!' I said again, panicking now. 'You've gone and killed her. You *idiots!*'

'What did you call me?' Guggs snarled.

'Calm down, freak,' Billy warned me. 'We haven't killed anyone.'

'Look at her!' I hissed. 'Her head's back to front! You think she's supposed to bend that way?'

'No, but—'

'What did you call me?' Guggs asked again, more slowly this time.

'Shut up,' I told him. A few weeks ago he would've terrified me, but now he was just Billy's brain-dead cousin with the stupid name. 'Just... shut up.'

'You tell him, kiddo,' Ameena smirked.

'Right, you're getting it,' he snarled. He took a step towards me, but Billy quickly put himself between us.

'She's not dead,' he said.

A flicker of surprise crossed Guggs' face, quickly replaced by a wicked grin. 'Oh, yeah, that's right. Forgot,' he said, slapping the iron bar against the palm of his hand. 'That's why I've got this.'

'Of course she's dead,' I said. The policewoman's body was a mangled mess, like a one-woman game of Twister. She *had* to be dead. Then again, I'd thought she'd been dead earlier too.

'Just watch,' Billy said, his voice hushed. The snow had eased off now. Just a few flakes drifted down from the sky.

All four of us fell silent as we watched the policewoman's body, and waited.

And waited.

And waited.

'I think she's actually *more* dead than she was a minute ago,' Ameena said. 'If that's possible.'

'Sssh! Shut up,' Billy hissed. He nodded towards the body. 'Just watch and... There. Did you see that?'

'See what?' I asked. 'I didn't see anything.'

'She moved.'

Ameena snorted. 'She didn't.'

Guggs changed his grip on the bar, holding it in both hands now, like a baseball batter about to hit a home run. 'Get ready,' he said quietly.

'Get ready for what?' I asked, but neither of them answered. The way Billy and Guggs were staring at the body, it was like they really, truly believed that—

'She moved.' It was Ameena who spoke. 'Her arm. There. See?'

And she was right. The policewoman's arm was moving,

bending at the elbow, getting into the push-up position. Her other arm was moving too. As it raised up, her hand bent fully back, revealing a broken stump of bone at her wrist.

'Told you,' Billy said, puffing out his chest.

'Who's the idiot now?' Guggs grunted. He took a sudden step towards the policewoman and raised the metal rod.

'Stop!' I cried. 'What are you doing?'

Guggs paused, mid-swing. 'Tell him, Bill.'

'Destroying the brain,' Billy explained.

I blinked. '"Destroying the brain"? What are you on about?'

'It's what you do, innit?' said Billy, shrugging. 'With zombies.'

I almost laughed. 'She's not a zombie.'

From down on the ground there was a *cracking* of bone. The policewoman gave a low groan as she tried to raise up on her broken legs.

'She does have certain... zombie qualities,' Ameena admitted. 'And she did try to eat you.'

The cousins turned on me. 'Did you get bit?' Guggs demanded, pointing the bar between my eyes.

'What? No! Shut up,' I scowled. 'She didn't bite me.'

'But she did try,' Ameena reminded me.

'Because she's a zombie,' Guggs said.

'Exactly,' Billy agreed. He gave his cousin a nod. 'Do it.'

Guggs raised the bar above his head. 'Destroy the brain!' he roared, cackling with glee.

'No,' I cried, feeling the sparks surge through me. By the time Guggs swung down, his hands were empty.

'What the hell? Where'd my pole go?'

Billy glared at me. His eyes narrowed, but he didn't say anything.

'No one's getting their brain destroyed,' I said. 'Whatever she is, she's still human. She's still a person.'

'It was there in my hand,' Guggs complained, searching the snow behind him for his missing weapon. 'Where'd it go?'

'OK. Well, what do we do with her, then?' Billy

demanded, stabbing a finger in the policewoman's direction.

I looked to Ameena. 'Your call,' she said, shrugging.

My breath came out as a big white cloud of mist, but I was too numb to feel the cold.

'Right,' I said, barely able to believe what I was about to do. 'I've got an idea.'

Chapter Seven

THE SCREECHERS

WHUM-WHUM-WHUM.

The windscreen wipers whipped back and forth, valiantly battling with the snow that had begun, once more, to fall. It was a battle they could never win. Caught in the headlights, the snowflakes looked like stars, whipping towards us, giving the impression the car was travelling at the speed of light.

It very much wasn't.

I leaned forward from the back seat. 'Can't you go any faster?'

Guggs gave a curt shake of his head. In the front passenger seat, Ameena rested her feet on the dashboard.

She'd claimed the front seat immediately, leaving me hunched in the back with Billy.

'Hey, give Huggs a break,' Ameena said. 'Twenty's plenty. Am I right, Huggs?'

'It's Guggs.'

'I think you suit Huggs better. You look like a Huggs kind of guy. You're Huggs now. That's that.'

A leery grin spread across Guggs' face. 'I can do a lot more than just hug. You ever been kissed by a real man, sweetheart?'

'You ever had your lungs ripped out through your eyes?' Ameena asked, smiling sweetly. 'Because it can be arranged.'

'I'd just like to get to wherever we're going a bit quicker,' I said. 'Considering what we've got in the boot.'

'A zombie,' Billy said.

I sat back in my seat, arms crossed over my chest. 'Whatever. Let's just get a move on.'

We drove on in silence for a while, the only sounds the

swishing of the wiper blades, the crunching of snow beneath the tyres and, I thought, a faint knocking coming from within the boot.

I wasn't sure what the penalty was for kidnapping a police officer – even a zombie one – but considering I was already wanted for murder and attempted murder, I suppose it couldn't really make things much worse.

'So.'

I turned to find Billy staring at me. 'So?' I replied.

'How's your stomach?'

Remembering the pain, my fingers felt for the spot where Billy's knife had punctured my belly. It had fully healed within hours – my abilities had seen to that – but I didn't want to let him know what had happened.

'Still hurts,' I lied. 'How's your ankle?'

He shrugged. 'Fine. Wasn't broken.'

Damn.

'Right,' I said. 'Well, maybe next time.'

He grunted and shook his head. 'Maybe.'

I thought that was the conversation over, but then he

surprised me. 'Sorry,' he said quietly. 'When I stabbed you, it... it wasn't me. It was like something got inside my head and made me do it. I couldn't stop myself.'

I nodded. Billy saying sorry – now there was something I never thought I'd hear. 'It's OK. It was a crazy day,' I said. 'How's Lily coping? Where is she?'

It bugged me that I cared about Billy's little sister, but then it was partly my fault she'd been caught up in the battle with Caddie and Raggy Maggie, her big brother's imaginary friends. Ameena and I had saved her, but I hadn't seen her again since.

He looked away then, turning his face to the window and gazing out at the blizzard of white beyond.

'Billy—?' I began, but a growl from the front passenger seat cut me off.

'Touch me again and I'll kill you,' Ameena said. 'Consider that fair warning.'

'Yeah, right,' Guggs smirked. 'I think you're complaining a bit too much. You're well into me.'

'My fist's going to be well into your face in a minute.'

'What's going on?' I demanded, leaning forward.

'Huggs just grabbed my leg,' Ameena said.

'He did *what*?' I spluttered.

'Wait...' Guggs said. 'You two? You're together?'

'What? No!' I said, a bit too loudly.

Ameena didn't answer. Why didn't she answer? Did she...?

'Come on, sweetheart, you can do better than him. Why not get with a real man?'

'You keep calling yourself that, but seriously, Huggs, real men don't drive at fifteen miles per hour.'

Even Billy laughed at that, though he made sure he did it quietly. Even so, rage flashed across the strip of Guggs' face I could see in the rear view mirror.

'Stop calling me Huggs!' he protested. His foot hit the floor and the car surged forward. I was thrown back into the seat as we began hurtling along the snow-covered street.

'Whoa, easy,' I complained, but Guggs didn't seem

to be listening. He was staring straight ahead now, gripping the wheel until his knuckles burned white.

There was a *whooshing* from beneath the wheels as the car slid sideways around a sharp corner. Guggs crunched down the gears and the engine whined loudly. With a sudden jolt we shot forward again, weaving from side to side as the wheels struggled to grip the snow.

'OK, Guggs,' Billy said, as he bounced against the side window. 'Point proved. Slow down, mate.'

'*Shut up, Billy,*' Guggs seethed. The wipers were *whumming* across the screen, but for all the good they were doing, we may as well have been driving blind. 'You want to see how a real man drives?' he said, scowling at Ameena. 'How's this?'

Ameena yawned. 'Sorry,' she said. 'I must've nodded off.'

'Stop winding him up!' I hissed, as we roared around another corner, spraying dirty slush in our wake. Outside, the snow streaked sideways past the windows, disappearing beyond the red glow of the car's tail lights. 'Guggs, stop the car. Cut it out.'

'What's the matter, you *scared*?' he sneered, grinding through the gears again. 'Too fast for you? What do you think of your boyfriend now, sweetheart?'

Ameena blinked. 'Whoops,' she said innocently. 'Must've fallen asleep again. Are we still moving?'

'Ameena!' I wailed, giving the back of her seat a shove.

'Guggs,' Billy cried. 'Come on, cuz, chill out!'

'I'll chill out when she stops playing hard to get,' Guggs snapped. 'What do you say, sweetheart?'

And that was when he went too far. That was when he grabbed Ameena's leg again.

The moment he made contact, she caught his thumb. He howled in agony as she bent it into his wrist, twisting his arm at the same time until it was bending up his back.

BAM.

His face hit the steering wheel hard enough to sound the horn. Out of control, the car lurched violently sideways. Even with my seatbelt on, I was thrown on top of Billy. He gave a pained hiss and clutched his lower leg. So, it seemed he hadn't completely healed up, after all.

As I leaned back to my own side, I caught sight of something in the darkness up ahead. Something large, solid, and half-buried by snow.

'Look out!' I cried, lunging for the steering wheel to try to change course. *'Car—'*

There was a noise then that I can't describe. Not a bang or a crash, but something more, as the front of our car ploughed into the back of one that was parked by the side of the road.

I slid towards the front until the seatbelt tightened across my chest. It slammed me back down, but my arms flailed out like a rag doll's and my head snapped sharply forward, then back.

There was a loud hissing sound and an airbag exploded

free of the steering wheel, pushing Guggs back into the driving seat.

The car spun, but the snow churning beneath the wheels quickly brought it to a full stop. For a moment there was no sound in the car but the unsteady rasping of our breathing.

'Now,' smiled Ameena, 'you cannot say that wasn't fun.'

'You idiot!' Billy cried. His face was as white as the snow on the windscreen. 'You could've killed us!'

'Not my fault,' Ameena said. She had released her grip on Guggs, who was now struggling with a slowly deflating airbag. 'I did warn him.' She turned to me. 'You heard me warn him, right?'

I nodded, too shaken to speak.

'There you go,' Ameena smiled. 'Like I said, wasn't my fault.'

'You're nuts,' Billy muttered. 'She's absolutely nuts.'

He and I both jumped as the alarm of the car we'd hit suddenly began to wail.

'We have to move,' Guggs grunted. I'd expected him

to have a go at Ameena, or even attack her, but he was already opening the door and climbing out past the half-filled airbag. 'Come on, Billy.'

Billy didn't wait to be told twice. He unclipped his seatbelt and opened the door in one move. A blast of icy air rushed into the car as he clambered outside.

'Where are you going?' I called after him. The door half-closed, then opened again.

'Can't hang around here,' Billy said, leaning down. 'Zombies aren't the only thing roaming around,' he finished, before the door slammed shut. I remembered the footprint in the sugar on Mrs Angelo's kitchen floor. From the look on Ameena's face, I could tell she was thinking the very same thing.

'What do you mean?' I asked, getting out of the car. Ameena got out too, and stood beside me. Billy and Guggs were already several paces away. Guggs had another metal bar in his hand now, shorter than the one he'd had before. I had to raise my voice to be heard over the car alarm. 'What else is there?'

They trudged on, moving slowly through the snow. I stumbled after them until Billy was less than an arm's length away. He twisted when my hand caught him by the shoulder, and spun to face me, fists raised. But the cocky, bullying, arrogant Billy wasn't there behind his eyes. There was nothing there but fear.

'Just keep moving,' he said, walking backwards.

I pointed back to the car, already hard to make out in the blizzard. 'What about her? In the boot? We can't just leave her.'

'Hurry up, Billy,' Guggs barked.

'What else is out there?' I asked again. 'What's—?'

A deep, rumbling roar rolled across the sky. It rose in pitch, becoming more like a screech before it finally faded away. Ameena was beside me again. 'What,' she asked, 'was that?'

Billy's reply came as a low and scratchy whisper. 'The Beast,' he said. 'It's the Beast.'

'Billy, come on!'

'The Beast? What's the Beast?' I asked.

'Explain later,' Billy said, turning and stumbling away. 'Need to get inside.'

'Now you're talking,' Ameena said. She caught me by the arm. 'Come on, let's get warm, then we can figure out what all the shenanigans are about.'

'*Jesus Christ!*'

Guggs' voice was shrill and panicked. I could just make him out in the gloom, swinging wildly with the metal bar.

'What's he doing?' I muttered, before I saw a shape making a wild lunge at him through the snowstorm. It was a man. I'd seen him around the village a few times, and at the supermarket in town. But I'd never seen him like this.

His eyes were coal black, his skin shades of grey. A mess of blood covered the bottom half of his face. It was smeared over his chin and down his neck, and it soaked into the thin white t-shirt he wore. On his bottom half he wore nothing but boxer shorts and socks. The boxers were marked with big red dots. From here,

I couldn't tell if the spots were a pattern, or if they were blood.

The man opened his mouth as he hurled himself at Guggs. His whole bottom jaw seemed to dislocate, turning the mouth into a gaping cavern, lined top and bottom with yellowing teeth.

For a second, I thought those teeth were going to clamp down on Guggs, but then Guggs' arm was swinging. The metal bar caught the man just above the ear. From several metres away I heard the sickening crunch of splintering bone.

But still the man kept coming. His hands reached for Guggs' clothes, grabbing at them, clawing at them, pulling the boy closer.

BANG! The metal bar hit him again, across the forehead this time. Blood spurted from the wound and flowed down into the man's eyes, blinding him.

But still he kept coming.

'Let go of me!' Guggs roared, delivering another blow to the man's head. The freakishly large mouth opened even wider, as he lunged again for Guggs' face.

'Oh, give me that,' Ameena sighed, snatching the bar away. Bending low, she swung with it. The man's knee gave an unpleasant *crack*, and then he was on the ground, still clawing and biting, but no longer able to stand.

Guggs looked at the length of metal as it was thrust back into his hand. 'See?' he mumbled. 'You do like me.'

'Not in a million years,' she told him, before she turned and strode towards me.

Halfway there she stopped as another squeal of rage shattered the quiet. Shapes moved through the snow all around us. They emerged from behind cars, from behind hedges, from behind walls. They staggered in our direction, flailing and screeching, eyes dark, faces stained with blood.

'Meet at the police station,' Billy said.

'What?'

'The police station,' he said, his voice shrill with rising panic. 'Meet there.'

The screeching and gnashing was all around us now. Fifteen, twenty or more of them, closing in, faster and faster. Guggs was already sprinting for a gap, iron bar raised, just in case. Some of the screechers were changing direction, trying to cut him off, but they'd never reach him in time.

Billy ran for another gap in the approaching circle of bodies, limping slightly. 'The police station,' he called back over his shoulder. 'Meet there, and whatever you do – do *not* get eaten!'

Chapter Eight

TRAPPED IN THE MAZE

More of the screechers chased after Billy, hissing and snarling as they lurched through the snow. That left at least eight or nine other figures still closing in on Ameena and me. And they were closing fast.

'This way,' I said, taking the lead. I made for the widest gap, keeping as much distance between myself and the screechers as possible. I half-ran, half-stumbled, but made it past the first of them without too much trouble.

But then a shape lunged at me from the left. I staggered right, avoiding the clawing swipe of an outstretched hand. Peggy, the woman who ran the local shop, came at me, gnashing her teeth until rivers of foamy saliva ran down her chin.

She would've caught me, too, had another flailing shape not thudded into her, sending them both crashing down into the snow. I didn't recognise the other person, but his dark eyes and blood-flecked face told me all I needed to know.

Peggy and the new arrival were up in a flash, howling and spitting as they resumed the chase. I raced on, hurdling the smaller snowdrifts, dragging my legs through the larger ones.

The air was a chorus of screams and roars, as more and more of the screechers broke cover. My heart thudded inside my chest. My leg muscles tightened with cold and with cramp. Despite protests from my brain, my body was slowing down, giving in to the cold.

A narrow path disappeared between two bungalows, dead ahead. If we could just reach it, maybe we could lose the screechers in the maze of lanes and alleyways behind the houses.

'Down here,' I panted, 'quick!'

The houses had shielded the path from the worst of the

snow, and the going was easier as soon as I reached it. I sped up, zig-zagging through the labyrinth of back gardens and passageways, listening out for footsteps behind me. I was relieved when I heard none, but the relief quickly faded.

I could hear no footsteps.

None.

I stopped at a junction between two paths. No footsteps. Not the screechers', and not Ameena's. I backtracked, searching the previous passageway, and the one before that, but she wasn't there. Ameena wasn't there.

'Ameena?' I said, as loudly as I dared. No reply came, except the soft *pit-a-pat* of the falling snow.

The next alleyway was boxed in by high wooden fences. I was halfway along it before I remembered the last time I'd been here. Ameena and I had hidden in one of these very gardens as Mr Mumbles hunted us down. The garage we'd become trapped in was somewhere nearby, and the police station not too far from that. I would get there and meet up with Billy, as per the plan. But not without Ameena.

I tried again, calling her name softly but hearing nothing back. I inched along the path, my breath clouding in front of my face, my feet crunching through the snow. I called again. No answer. *Where was she?*

The path turned to the right up ahead. I pressed my back against the high fence and side-stepped up to the corner. Slowly, I leaned around it, twisting my neck to peek along the alleyway.

Gaaaagh.

I leaned back out of sight, already feeling my pulse quickening. There were two of them standing just four or five metres along the path. Had they seen me? Probably. Maybe. I had no idea. I held my breath, kept as still as I could, listening for any sign of movement.

They moaned a few times. Their feet shuffled back and forth through the snow. But there were no screams or howls to suggest they knew I was there.

Being even more cautious this time, I stole a look along

the path. The two figures were no closer than they had been, but they were no further away either. They shambled from side to side across the path, bumping into one of the fences, then turning and shuffling back until they collided with the one opposite.

I watched them for a few moments, trying to figure out what to do next. This was the way I'd run, but they were blocking the path. If I wanted to get back to Ameena, I'd have to find another route.

With a final glance at the two men, I quietly turned away from the corner. Peggy from the shop stood a metre or less away. With a strangled cry she lumbered towards me, arms raised. I jumped back, but the fence was behind me. Her hands caught me by the shoulders. I felt her fingernails dig into my skin, watched helplessly as her mouth dropped open and she let out a piercing scream.

The fence behind me shook violently. I looked up to see another screecher clambering over it from the other side. Her spindly arms lashed out, grabbing for my hair, or for any other part of me they could reach.

Two more voices howled behind me as the men I'd been watching staggered along the path, their hands clawing for me, their jaws munching in hungry anticipation.

'Get... off,' I grimaced, pushing Peggy back. She was stronger than she looked, though, and her grip didn't slip from my shoulder. Her mouth opened wider. She leaned in. I saw her black tongue, smelled nothing but death on her breath.

I drove my knee into her stomach. Once. Twice. She hissed at me from the back of her throat. Her teeth snapped shut just centimetres from my nose. *Clack-clack.*

Rough hands grabbed my face from behind, pulling me back. I twisted, pulled free, and fired an elbow sharply backwards. It hit something soft and fleshy, doing the attacking screecher no harm at all.

I yelped in pain as the fingers of the one on the fence finally found my hair. She pulled up sharply, trying to lift me off the ground and claim me for her own. Until then,

I'd been keeping a lid on my panic, but that was the moment the lid came off.

The power buzzed at the base of my skull. 'Don't kill them!' I begged, not quite sure who I was saying it to. And then sparks exploded inside my head.

The wooden fences on either side of me snapped and splintered. An invisible force batted the screechers away. They twisted and hissed as they were hurled through the air in every direction. The snow at my feet was blown up into the air, surrounding me in a cloud of dusty white.

The screechers landed on their backs in piles of dirty snow, but they were back on their feet almost right away. Their black eyes glared at me, their mouths still gnashing at nothing.

I spun around. The paths were blocked in every direction. My powers were tingling through me, waiting to be put to use again, but until I was sure of the consequences of using them, they were a last resort.

The woman who'd caught me by the hair was half-buried beneath the remains of the fence she'd been on.

She was thrashing around, struggling to free herself. I leapt over her and landed in the garden of a mid-terrace house. The back door stood open. I dashed towards it, tripping and stumbling through the snow. The screechers scrambled after me. They were faster than I was, but I had a head start.

I reached the door and fell inside, landing on the kitchen lino with a *thud*. Rolling on to my back I kicked the door as hard as I could. It slammed closed just as Peggy bounded up the step. I heard the *crunch* of the wood hitting her face, then the squeal of wounded rage that followed.

The door shook as Peggy and the others hurled themselves against it. They scratched and clawed as I got up and looked around the kitchen.

'Key. *Key!*' Frantically, I searched the worktops and the windowsill. 'Come *on*, there's got to be – yes!'

I spotted the key, already in the lock. My fingers trembled as I wrestled with it, trying to get it turned. At last, with a faint *click*, I managed to secure the door. Outside, the screechers were still trying to batter it down, but I reckoned it would keep them out. For now, at least, I was safe.

Assuming, of course, there wasn't already one in the house with me.

On the other side of the kitchen, the door leading through to the living room was shut tight. I approached it quietly and pressed my ear against the wood. With the racket the screechers were making outside, it was virtually impossible to tell if there was any noise from the room beyond this door. There was only one way to know for sure.

I pulled the door open a crack but was ready to slam it closed again if I had to. The living room was a mess. A couch lay on its back, its torn cushions spilling their stuffing out all over the floor. The frame of a coffee table stood in the middle of the room, its glass top shattered into diamond-like shards on the carpet.

Opening the door all the way, I stepped into the room and saw the full extent of the damage. Three deep gouges ran almost the full length of one wall. They tore through the wallpaper and through the plaster beneath. I poked my finger into one of the grooves. It sunk in right up to the third knuckle.

I remembered the footprint we'd found in Mrs Angelo's house. I looked at the claw marks along the wall. More than anything, I tried not to think about what could be responsible for both.

There were two windows at opposite ends of the room, the curtains drawn over both. I decided to leave them that way, rather than risk attracting the attention of anyone else outside.

A second door in the living room stood wide open. Through it, I could see the house's front door – closed, thankfully – and the first step of a staircase leading to the upper floor.

I made for the stairs. I could peek through a bedroom window and get a better idea of what was going on outside, hopefully without being noticed by anyone down on the ground.

At the bottom step I hesitated, one hand gripping the

banister, the other pressed against the opposite wall. I stood there in silence, listening for any sound from above.

Nothing.

'Hello?' I said. 'Anyone there?'

Again, nothing.

Placing my feet at the outside edges of each step to minimise creaking, I crept up to the top of the stairs. Four doors led off from the upper landing. Three of them were open, one wasn't. I looked in the first three rooms, but found nothing of interest in any of them.

One of the bedrooms overlooked the back garden. Blinds were closed over the narrow window. I eased two of the metal strips apart just enough to allow me to see out.

The first thing I noticed was that the snow had stopped falling. The next thing I noticed were the screechers. The garden was full of them now. I counted fifteen before I stopped and came away from the window. Going out through the back door was out of the question. That was all I needed to know.

Out front, the picture was brighter. I kept low behind the curtains of the second bedroom, looking out on to the main street. There were two screechers out there from what I could see, both well apart and shuffling in opposite directions.

Through the window I could see almost the whole route to the police station. It looked like it was completely clear. A straight sprint and I could reach it in just a few minutes, as long as the snow didn't slow me down too much.

I decided that was what I would do. I'd get to the police station and meet up with the others. If I knew Ameena, she'd probably have headed there the moment we got separated. It would've been the sensible thing for her to do, and when it came to staying alive, Ameena was the most sensible person I'd ever met.

Feeling suddenly hopeful, I left the bedroom and headed for the stairs. But a sound from beyond the closed door stopped me in my tracks. It was a soft padding sound – footsteps on carpet – and the high-pitched squeak of a creaky floorboard.

I stepped back towards the stairs, getting ready to run as the handle turned and the bedroom door was opened from the inside.

'Hello, son,' said a man whose face I now knew all too well. My dad ran his fingers through his dark shaggy hair and flashed me a shark-like smile. 'Long time no see.'

Chapter Nine

BLAME IT ON BABY

The last time I'd seen my dad, I'd smashed a rock into the side of his head. He hadn't liked that much.

I could still see a yellow-black bruise that ran across his temple and around one eye. The bruising seemed to bulge the eye outwards, making him look more deranged than ever.

'*You*,' I gasped. 'What are you doing here?'

'Just checking up on you,' he said. 'Making sure you're OK. What kind of father would I be if I didn't check up on you every once in a while?'

He flashed me another smile, then turned and marched into the back bedroom. I held off for a moment, considering making a run for it and taking my chances with the screechers. But I had a lot of questions, and there was a very good chance he held the answers.

'Quite a day, huh?' he said as I entered the bedroom. He pulled the drawstring next to the window and the metal blinds rolled all the way up. He leaned on the sill and looked down at the garden, then whistled quietly through his teeth. 'Quite a day.'

'You did this,' I said. 'Didn't you? You caused all this.'

He turned from the window and leaned his back against the glass. 'Me? No. Wouldn't know where to start. But you have to admire the handiwork. The whole village? Wiped out in one night?' He blew out his cheeks. 'You have to admire the handiwork.'

I stood my ground as he stepped towards me. 'Oh, sure, there are a few survivors. A few stragglers still hanging around, but they'll get them. Those things out there are nothing if not persistent. Am I right?'

'Where's my nan?' I demanded.

'I don't have the first clue.'

'Don't lie!' I snapped. 'Where is she?'

'My *guess*? She's out there somewhere.' He jabbed a thumb towards the window. 'All black-eyed and chomping teeth.' He lunged towards me and clacked his teeth together just centimetres from the tip of my nose. I flinched and pulled back, which made him laugh out loud. 'Sorry,' he said. 'Couldn't resist.'

'I swear, if you've hurt her...' I told him.

He waved a hand dismissively and sat on the end of the unmade bed. 'So,' he began. 'How's things?'

I gawped at him. 'What?'

'How's things? How's life been treating you?'

'Sorry... are you *mental*?' I asked.

'What? I'm just asking how you've been. What's so bad about that? We're bonding here.'

'No,' I growled. 'We aren't.'

'Ah, suit yourself,' he said, and he went back to looking out of the window.

'What are you doing here?' I asked him. 'What do you want?'

He shrugged. 'Some father–son time, that's all. Not too much to ask, is it?'

'Yes,' I replied, coldly, 'it is. What, you think after everything you've done you can just drop in for a cosy chat whenever you feel like it? It doesn't work that way.'

'After everything I've done?' he said, looking genuinely puzzled. 'Why, what have I done?'

I almost choked. 'What do you...? What have you...?' I began counting things off on my fingers. 'You sent Mr Mumbles after me. You sent Caddie after me. You sent the Crowmaster, and because of that my mum is in hospital and Marion is dead.'

'Whoa, back up. That's not my fault,' he said, holding up his hands. 'You could've protected them if you'd wanted to.'

'What? No I couldn't!'

'Of course you could, kiddo. With your abilities you can do anything you want.' He gave a sad shake of his head. 'Maybe deep down you just didn't want to save them, after all.'

'Shut up,' I warned him.

'What's the point in being *special* if you don't put your talents to use?' he asked, breaking into a smile. 'You could've saved them. You could've saved *everyone*. But no, you just flail around, too scared to realise your real potential. It's a shame. It's a damn shame.'

'I know what you're doing,' I said. 'The Crowmaster told me everything. He told me exactly why you want me to use my abilities, and he told me what would happen if I did.'

The grin stayed fixed on my dad's face, but his eyes told another story. 'Yes,' he said. 'You mentioned that.' He pointed to the bruise on his face. 'Just before you gave me this, remember? What exactly did he say?'

'That you want to bring the Darkest Corners over here into this world. And you need me to do it. The more I use my powers, the weaker the barrier between the worlds becomes. That's right, isn't it? He was telling the truth.'

To my surprise, he didn't deny it. 'Yes, son, the scarecrow was telling the truth,' he said. 'You might as well know. No harm in it. It's not like you can stop it now, anyway. Every time you use your... *gift*, the doorway between this world and mine opens a little further. Use it enough, and we can all go free.'

'You're already free.'

'Temporarily,' he sighed. 'Only temporarily. And, believe it or not, I'm not just thinking about me. I'm not the only one trapped over there, you know?'

'Yeah, I know,' I said. 'You sent some to visit me, remember?'

'I don't mean those... *things*,' he spat. 'I mean normal people. Good people. Kids, even, all doing their best to hide out and stay alive.'

Immediately, I thought of I.C., the boy I'd found hiding in the hospital in the Darkest Corners. He had been scared and alone, but try as I might, I couldn't bring him back with me to the real world. I'd had no choice but to leave him there, although I had – I hoped – arranged for him to be looked after.

'You can help them, son. You can help all of them get out. They'd be safe.'

'They'd bring all the monsters with them,' I said. 'They wouldn't be safe. *No one* would be safe.'

He threw back his head and laughed. 'OK, you got me,' he cackled. 'I couldn't give a damn about any of them. Let the freaks tear every last one of them to pieces, what do I care?'

'Then why are you doing all this?' I asked.

His laughter stopped. 'Everything I do, son – every *single* thing I've done for the past decade – I've done for one reason and one reason only.' He looked me up and down, his face a mask of contempt. 'To hurt you.'

I'm not sure why, but tears suddenly stung my eyes. I blinked them back. There was no way I was about to give him the satisfaction. 'Why?' I asked, hoping he didn't hear the wobble in my voice.

'Why?' he shouted, flying at me. This time, I managed to stand my ground. '*Why?* Because it's your fault I got sent to that place, that's why. Fourteen years I've been stuck there, with the freaks and the demons coming for me every night! Fourteen *years*.'

'I wasn't even born fourteen years ago,' I protested.

His hand caught me by the throat. My back slammed against the bedroom wall. 'No, but you were *going* to be,' he hissed. 'You were *going to be*.'

He relaxed his grip and stepped away. When he spoke again his voice was distant, as if he barely remembered I was even in the room. 'She was so lonely, your mum. No friends. Just her *own* mother for company.'

Sounds familiar, I thought, but I kept quiet.

'We found each other. She needed... *someone*. And I needed her to keep me out of that place. Getting her to fall in love with me was easy. She was eighteen, not bad looking, but no one had ever paid her the slightest bit of attention before then. I had her eating out of my hand in no time.'

'You used her,' I said, through gritted teeth.

His face darkened. 'And then we found out we were going to have a little baby. And suddenly she didn't need me to make her feel special any more. All of a sudden, she had someone else to love.'

'Me,' I realised.

He nodded. 'You. Next thing I know I'm in the Darkest Corners, fighting for my life, while she's out buying prams and knitting bootees. So tell me, son,' he spat, 'who used who?'

'She thought you left her,' I said weakly.

'Left her? I'd have stayed with her forever.' He shook his head. 'I didn't *leave* her, she sent me away.'

'But... none of that was my fault! I didn't do anything.'

He narrowed his eyes. 'You know what? You're right. You've done nothing wrong. You're the innocent in all this. I should be taking it out on her.'

'No!' I cried, stepping forward. 'Don't!'

'I *could* have just killed you. That would've been easier. I could've ended you any time I liked, but after everything I've had to go through because of you, killing you just didn't seem enough.'

He knocked on the window and gave a cheerful wave

down towards the back garden. Even through the glass, I heard the screechers begin to howl and batter harder against the door.

'I wanted you to suffer. Physically, obviously, but mentally too. I wanted you to be scared, like I was. And I wanted you all churned up and twisted with guilt over the people you let die.'

I cleared my throat. 'Well,' I said. 'Mission accomplished.'

'Oh no, son,' he smirked, 'trust me, you haven't seen *anything* yet. You think you feel bad now? Just wait until you open that doorway for me. Just wait until you spill the blood of every man, woman and child in this world.'

'That's not going to happen,' I insisted. Now that I knew for sure the Crowmaster had been telling the truth, the decision was easy. 'I won't use my abilities again.'

His face twisted with rage. '*I'll* decide what you do and don't do with your abilities. Me! What, you think you got those powers from your mother's side? They're all me, kiddo. I gave you them, and you'll damn well use them, even if I have to make you.'

'You won't make me,' I replied. 'Whatever you send after me, I'll find a way to beat it without using my powers.'

He raised an eyebrow and snorted. 'Really?' he said. 'Good luck with that. The fact is, they're part of you. You can no more stop using them than you can stop your fingernails from growing.'

'I won't,' I insisted. 'I swear.'

He rummaged in his pocket, eventually pulling out a small, hand-held tape recorder. 'Well, if it comes to it, maybe this will change your mind,' he said.

'What's that?'

He slipped the machine back in his pocket. 'Insurance.'

A movement in the corridor behind me made me turn. A figure in a brown robe stood on the landing. A hood was down over the figure's head, hiding his face. I'd seen this person a few times now, always lurking in the shadows near my dad. He never lifted the hood and never spoke a word. I wasn't even sure if he was even a "he" at all.

My dad pushed past me, making for the door. Just

inside the room he stopped, as if a thought had only just occurred to him. 'Your friend,' he said. 'Ameena, is it?'

'What about her?'

'How much do you actually know about her?' he asked.

I didn't hesitate, not even for a second. 'I know enough. I know that I trust her.'

A smile tugged at the corners of his mouth. 'Interesting,' he nodded. 'See you around.'

And then he was stepping out of the room, pulling the door behind him.

'What's that supposed to mean?' I demanded, racing after him. But by the time I made it out on to the landing, neither my dad nor the figure in brown were anywhere to be seen. 'Great,' I mumbled. 'Just great.'

What *had* he meant? Of course I could trust Ameena. She'd saved my life countless times. Without her, I'd have died on my front step, with Mr Mumbles kneeling on my chest. Or, if not then, then a hundred times since. The fact I was even breathing was all down to Ameena. I owed her everything.

Pushing my dad's question from my mind, I took another look at the situation beyond the front windows. The snow was still off, and the street was completely empty now. The two screechers I'd seen earlier seemed to have stumbled away somewhere, leaving the route to the police station completely clear.

I took the stairs two at a time. There was a row of jackets hanging on the wall beside the front door. I found a warm one in about my size and pulled it on.

After zipping up, I stopped at the door just long enough to take a deep, steadying breath. My hand pushed down on the handle and the door slowly opened.

Right then, I thought. *Here goes nothing.*

'What do you mean, "she's not here"?'

Billy spun the office chair he was sitting on a full three-hundred-and-sixty degrees, then leaned back with his hands behind his head. On the other side of the police station's reception area, Guggs knelt by the window, looking out.

The journey from the house to the police station had

gone perfectly smoothly. I'd actually laughed with relief as I'd arrived at the front door and banged on it until Billy let me inside.

I wasn't laughing now.

'She's not here,' Billy repeated. 'I thought she was with you?'

'No, she isn't,' I said.

I turned from the desk and hurried back towards the door I'd just come through. From the corner of my eye, I saw Guggs stand up.

'Where are you going?' he asked. 'You can't go back out. You know what's out there.'

'Yes,' I nodded. 'My friend. And I'm going to find her.'

'You're not going anywhere,' Guggs told me. He pointed at me with his metal bar. 'We stick together. Strength in numbers. You go and you're putting us at risk. Tell him, Bill.'

Billy looked at his cousin, then back at me. He stood up and took something from the desk behind him. I looked down at the walkie-talkie as he pressed it into my hand.

'Keep it on,' he said. 'If she turns up, we'll let you know.'

I clipped the radio to my belt. 'Thanks,' I said.

Billy nodded his head, just barely. 'Good luck,' he said. 'Make sure you come back.'

'I will,' I said. I turned to the door, then hesitated. 'One thing. What's the Beast?'

Billy shrugged. 'Don't know. Haven't seen it. Just seen what it can do.'

'Like what?' I asked.

He swallowed hard. 'Trust me,' he said, his voice a hoarse whisper. 'You don't want to know.'

There was a story there, I knew, something Billy wasn't telling me. It could wait. Ameena couldn't.

'Fair enough,' I said, then I opened the door, pulled my jacket around my neck, and stepped back out into the harsh, biting cold.

Chapter Ten

THE NOT-SO-SUPERMARKET

I scampered, crouched-over, across to the scene of our earlier car smash, keeping my eyes peeled for trouble. The lights of the vehicle we'd hit were still flashing, but the alarm had long since stopped. There were no screechers around the crash-scene, but there was no Ameena, either.

I squatted down by the car we'd been in. Aside from the now almost deflated airbag, everything was just as we'd left it – keys in the ignition, engine running, three of the four doors standing wide open. If Ameena had come back to the car, she'd left no trace behind.

Keeping low, I crept down to the back of the vehicle and knelt in the snow beside it.

Ahead of me, I could see the entrance to the maze of alleys I'd run into. I wondered if the screechers were still there, still banging against the locked door of the house, trying to get inside.

They didn't seem to be very smart, but I doubted even they would stay there forever. They'd come looking for us soon enough, which was why I kept out of sight behind the car until I could figure out my next move.

The last time I'd seen Ameena had been here. She'd got out of the car at the same time as I had. We'd watched Guggs and Billy make a bolt for it, then I'd run off, assuming she was right behind me.

I cast my eyes over the snow around the car. No blood, other than a patch a dozen or so metres away, where Guggs had fought the screecher. We'd left the man lying on the ground with a shattered knee, but now there was no sign of him. Presumably he'd crawled off towards the alleyway, following the others.

So, the screechers were more or less accounted for, but Ameena? That was another matter.

I looked at the houses around me. 'Where *are* you?' I whispered.

A sudden *thump* from inside the boot made me jump. *The policewoman!* I'd forgotten she was even in there, somehow still alive. For a moment, I considered checking on her. But only for a moment, and even then, not seriously. Having seen close-up what the screechers were like, I knew that letting another one out would be a very stupid move.

THUMP. THUMP. THUMP.

She banged again on the inside of the boot, each strike harder than the one before. Dead or not, she was bloody determined.

THUMP. THUMP. CLANK!

The frosty paintwork creased like paper as a powerful blow hammered against it. A raised imprint of a clenched fist buckled the boot lid. I fell back as another dent appeared in the metal, then another, and another. The lid began to pull away from the body of the car. An eye flashed in the gap, black and bulging, before two rows of gnashing teeth took its place.

The whole car started shaking, squeaking as it rocked back and forth. Inside the boot, the policewoman thrashed around as she fought to force her way free. A piercing scream emerged from within the boot. It was muffled, but still loud enough to attract attention.

'*Ssh!*' I whispered, backing away. 'Shut up!'

The bent metal buckled further as more blows were rained upon it from the inside. Another scream, this one even louder than the one before, came through the widening gap. Somewhere not too far away, other screechers howled in response.

'Kyle!'

The voice came at me through a hiss of static. I almost screamed myself, before I remembered the walkie-talkie on my belt. 'Come in, Kyle. You there? Over.'

I fumbled the radio free, then pushed down on the talk button. 'I'm here,' I whispered, my eyes never leaving the battered boot of the car. 'What is it?'

Silence.

'What is it?' I asked again.

'You need to say "over",' Billy told me. 'Over.'

I bit down on the radio in sheer frustration. This was no time for walkie-talkie lessons. 'I don't care!' I hissed. '*What do you want?*'

More static, then Billy spoke again. 'Right, fine. Guggs has been up on the roof. He thinks he saw your girlfriend. Over.'

'On the roof?'

'No, not on the roof, you moron,' Billy sneered. 'At the shop. He was on the roof when he saw someone moving around at the shop. Over.'

I was already running, leaving the car and the policewoman behind, racing as fast as I could towards the village shop.

'And it was definitely her?' I asked.

A pause. Another hiss of static. 'You should really say "over", or it's hard to know when you're done talking. Over.'

'*Billy*, was it definitely her?'

'Not definitely her, no, but definitely *someone*. Over.'

'Right,' I said, turning on to the street where the shop was. 'I'll let you know.'

I clipped the radio back to my belt. After a moment, I clicked the switch that turned it off. There could be anything waiting for me in the shop. The last thing I needed was Billy's squawking voice giving me away.

The shop was at the far end of the street, right on the corner where this road met the next one. The street was deserted. I jogged along in the middle of the road. It made me visible to anything lurking nearby, but it also meant I'd have plenty of warning if something decided to come running at me.

Fortunately, nothing did. In no time, I was standing outside the shop. The sign above the door called it a "Supermarket", but there was nothing super about it.

The whole shop area was barely as large as my living room and kitchen combined. There were two rows of shelves in the middle of the floor, creating three very narrow aisles that ran almost the full length of the building. On a good day, the shelves were half empty. On an average day, it was more like three-quarters.

At the back of the shop, a set of swing doors led through to the store room. I'd only been through there once, when I was much younger and needed to use the shop's toilet. It was, if memory served, even more grim than the shop itself, with scratched and rusty metal shelving units and boxes stacked on every available surface.

The shop's main door and window were set back into the wall, creating a little outside alcove area where the two supermarket-style trolleys were stored. I used to wonder why there weren't more of them, until I realised the narrow aisles couldn't handle any more traffic than that without a major pile-up happening.

Only one trolley was parked outside when I approached the window. The rotting paintwork of the wooden frame was rough beneath my fingers as I crouched down and peeked in through the grimy glass.

The shop looked no more or less messy than usual.

There were wire baskets on the floor, but then there were always wire baskets on the floor. A cage stood at the far end of the middle aisle, stacked with boxes of crisps, washing powder, eggs, and more.

There was no blood. No bodies. No chaos. The shop looked like the shop always did – just a bit sort of... crap, really.

Confident there were no screechers inside, I approached the door. The handle turned without any problem, and I pushed the door open.

DING-A-LING!

The cheerful tinkle of the bell above the doorframe almost made my heart stop. The counter where Peggy stood to serve the customers was right in front of the window. I dived behind it, taking cover in case anything should come crashing through from the back store room.

I knelt there, down by the till rolls and the "Caution: Wet Floor" sign, listening to my breath rasping in and out. *Idiot.* I should've remembered the bell. If anyone was in here, then they knew I was here too.

But nothing happened in the shop to suggest anyone *was* here. Nothing moved along the aisles. Nothing charged through the store-room doors. Nothing at all.

I had just stood up when the *hissing* of radio static made me duck back down. I grabbed for the walkie-talkie. It was halfway to my ear before I remembered it was switched off.

The static continued to crackle. I searched around, eventually finding an old hi-fi system hidden behind a small sliding door beneath the till. It was switched to radio mode, but the numbers on the LED display were whirring past as it tried to pick up a signal to lock on to.

With a press of the big round power button, I switched it off. The static hiss died away, leaving the shop in silence once again. By leaning left and right at the till, I could see that all three aisles were clear. There were no screechers along any of them, and no Ameena either. All there was was the other trolley. It was down at the far end of the middle aisle, stacked high with items.

So, there was nothing interesting in the front shop,

but there was still the store room. My hope of finding Ameena here was fading fast, but I had to at least go and check to see if she was through the back somewhere.

Creeping out from behind the counter, I made my way along the right-hand aisle where the frozen food was kept. I was barely past the fish fingers when the speaker on the wall above me hissed and spat.

I stopped and stared up at it, listening to the sound of radio static. A voice suddenly crackled from within the speaker. It was broken up and distorted at first, but then the radio locked on to the station and the shop was filled with a chillingly familiar tune.

If you go down to the woods today, you're sure of a big surprise...

I felt my arms goosebump, as my skin turned as cold as the fish fingers beside me. No. No, it couldn't be.

If you go down to the woods today, you'd better go in disguise...

That song. It was *that song*. But... how?

For every bear that ever there was, will gather there for certain because...

How many times had I heard that song? How many times had Doc Mortis played it to me when I was trapped in his hospital in the Darkest Corners? Although the more pressing question was...

Today's the day the Teddy Bears have their picnic.

...why was it playing now?

I ran back to the till and punched the hi-fi's power button. The display went dark and the song was cut short halfway through the next line. I watched the little display screen, counting in my head.

I had just reached "three" when the stereo system lit up again. The numbers on the frequency display rolled past. Then they came to an abrupt stop and a DJ's voice chattered over the speakers.

'...keep your requests coming in,' he urged. 'Got one here that's just come through.'

My thumb was on the button again, about to switch it off, when the DJ stopped me.

153

'It's a message for Kyle Alexander,' he chirped, 'and it says "Not long now, kiddo". Bit cryptic, that one. And that comes from... who's that from? Where's my—? Here it is, that's from Kyle's dad, and he's asked us to play this. It's *Firestarter* by—'

The radio shut itself off. I stared at the display, half-expecting it to kick in again, but the speakers stayed silent this time. Still, I was shaking as I approached the door leading to the store room. How had he turned the radio on? How had he turned it to that station just as his message to me was read out?

And why make it play *The Teddy Bears' Picnic*? After everything I'd been through at the hands of Doc Mortis, just the thought of that song made my blood run cold through my veins. Had he played it to scare me? Or to tell me that Doc Mortis was somehow still alive?

A clatter from the back store pushed these thoughts from my mind, though. I was already crouching behind the counter, out of sight. I stayed there, looking around me for a weapon as the store-room doors swung open at the other end of the aisle.

Footsteps shuffled across the vinyl-covered floor. The wheels of the abandoned trolley began to *squeak*, reminding me of another trolley – the hospital trolley I'd been strapped to by Doc Mortis and his porters.

My heart began to race and my throat tightened, making breathing difficult. The footsteps and the *squeaking* were steadily drawing closer. No longer worried about drawing attention to myself now, I rummaged through the cupboards below the till, searching for something – anything – to defend myself with.

My fingers brushed against something metal. I grabbed it and stood up, holding my newly-acquired weapon out in front of me, ready to... to...

I looked at the object in my hand. Then I looked at Ameena, who was standing on the other side of the till.

'Nice stapler,' she said.

I let my hand fall back to my side. 'Where the hell did you go?' I demanded.

'Here,' she said, 'obviously. And don't worry, I've checked it over, there's no one else here.' She pointed to the laden trolley. 'I was getting supplies. Food and stuff.'

I scowled. 'What for?'

'Well, you know. So we don't starve.'

'Yes, but...' I shook my head. 'You could have told me. I thought you were behind me.'

'I did tell you,' she protested. 'I shouted after you, but you were screaming too loud to hear me.'

'I wasn't screaming!' I said.

'You *so* were,' she smirked. 'Like a thirteen-year-old girl at a pop concert.'

I felt myself blush. 'Yeah, well... I *am* a thirteen-year-old.'

'But you're not at a pop concert,' she pointed out. 'Or a girl.' Her eyes went past me and her face fell. 'Did you leave the door open?'

I turned and looked. The door stood halfway open. I'd left it like that when the bell had rung, deciding that getting to cover was more important than closing it behind me.

'Must've done,' I said. 'Is it a problem?'

'Probably not,' she shrugged. 'But come on, let's load up and get out of here.'

I looked at her trolley. 'I thought you already were loaded up?'

'I was,' she said. 'But now you're here, we can take twice as much.'

'Right,' I said. I started towards the door. 'I'll go get the other trolley.'

'No, wait,' Ameena said. She smiled and looked pleased with herself. 'I've got a better idea.'

Chapter Eleven

DAMSEL IN DISTRESS

'This is never going to work.'

Ameena turned to me and tutted. 'Yes, it will. It's genius.'

I lifted another few boxes from the shopping cart and took them outside. 'I don't see why we can't just leave everything in the trolley.'

'Because we can't push the trolley through the snow,' she said, stepping aside to let me back into the shop. As I picked up another bundle of supplies, she dumped her armful down on top of the plastic sledge she'd found in the store room. 'This one's nearly full,' she said. 'I'll go and get another one. You keep watch.'

I sat the boxes down on the counter and looked out

through the shop window. There had been no more snow, but the sky was thick with dark cloud. A mist seemed to be creeping its way through the village too, making it difficult to see more than a dozen metres or so in any direction. It would make our journey back to the police station difficult. And it'd make finding Nan even more so.

'Right, here we are,' Ameena said, barging through the swing doors. 'I got you a nice pink one. I thought you'd appreciate...'

She stopped walking and stopped talking at the same time. She stood midway along the third aisle, the sledge in her arms, not moving.

'What is it?' I asked. 'What's the matter?'

'I heard something,' she said quietly. 'I heard something moving.'

'It was probably just me,' I ventured, trying to convince myself as much as her.

Ameena shook her head. She was staring down at the gap beneath the shelving unit that ran along the wall. Little metal legs held the unit up at metre-wide intervals, but otherwise there was nothing but dark, empty space below the bottom shelf.

'It was from over here somewhere,' she whispered. She held the sledge out. 'Here, come and hold this.'

Reluctantly, I moved to join her, keeping my distance from the shelves she was looking at. The sledge felt light and flimsy as I took it from her. It wasn't until it slipped in my hand that I realised my palms were slick with sweat.

'Is it one of *them*?' I asked, my voice hushed.

'Dunno,' Ameena replied. 'But it's something.'

'I thought you said you checked the place over when you got here?' I said.

'I did,' she nodded. 'But then someone left the front door open.' She shot me an accusing glare, then slowly knelt down, first on to one knee, and then the other.

'What are you doing?' I hissed.

'Taking a look.'

'Why?'

'Why not?'

I began to list off all the reasons why not, but she was

already crouching down, crawling closer to the dark gap until her hands were beneath the shelves and her head was close behind.

'Crumbs, it's dark,' she muttered. 'But I don't think there's anything here.' She slid forward, until her head and shoulders were lost in the gloom. 'Nah, it looks OK.'

I smiled, relieved. 'Well, that's—'

'*Wait.*'

I waited, expecting her to say more. But she didn't. 'What is it?' I asked, suddenly nervous again.

'There's... I think there's something...'

A strangled cry of shock from Ameena sent me stumbling into the shelves behind me. Tins and packets rained down on the hard floor as, at my feet, Ameena's legs began to thrash around.

'Help!' she yelped. 'Kyle, help me! Pull me out!'

I babbled something incoherent and grabbed her by the ankles. She was still kicking and squirming as I dragged her free of the gap, but her screams had stopped.

I let go of her legs as she rolled on to her back.

Suddenly annoyed, I stood up and folded my arms across my chest.

'I hate you sometimes,' I told her.

She could barely speak for laughing. 'I don't know why I keep doing that,' she giggled. Tears were running down her face and her whole body was shaking with laughter. 'It's just, you keep falling for it! Every time.'

'I'm glad you think it's funny,' I scowled, watching her get back to her feet. 'One of these days I'm going to have a heart attack.'

That just set her off again. Her face creased and she doubled over, holding her sides. I stood there, arms folded, not saying another word until she finally straightened up and wiped her eyes on her sleeve.

'Oh,' she breathed. 'That was brilliant.'

'I'm glad you think so,' I said. 'I thought you were in trouble.'

She stopped herself laughing, but couldn't keep the smile away from her face. 'Sorry,' she said. 'Bad joke.'

'Yes, it was,' I nodded. 'Did you actually hear anything, or was the whole thing just one big wind-up?'

'No, I did hear something,' she shrugged. 'That bit was real, but it was probably just a—'

The hands that shot out from beneath the shelves, they were real too. I saw them for a fraction of a second, and then they were around Ameena's ankles. She didn't cry out, just looked sort of puzzled as her bottom half was dragged backwards, sending the rest of her falling forwards on to the floor.

Her hands slapped the scuffed vinyl, trying to get a grip, but the hold on her legs tightened and she was dragged further into the darkness beneath the shelves.

'Get off!' she growled, trying to kick at her attacker. But the shelving unit was too low, making it impossible for her to move her legs enough to stick the boot in. 'Let go of me!'

I caught her by the wrists. Her eyes met mine and I pulled. Whatever was holding on to her was strong. I planted my feet and leaned backwards, using my weight and all my strength to drag her free of the shelves.

Finally, I managed to get her all the way out. But she didn't come out alone.

The screecher who had attacked Guggs at the crash scene had a hand around each of her ankles. His jaw dropped open and he lunged for her legs. She tried to kick, but her legs were pinned beneath him. His mouth looked wide enough to swallow the rest of his head. His black eyes glistened as his teeth began to clamp shut.

THUNK!

I rammed the end of the sledge between his jaws and his teeth bit into the pink plastic. Roaring with the effort, I shoved the sledge hard. His head bent backwards until I was sure his neck would snap. I pushed again and this time his grip slipped from Ameena's ankles. She scrambled free just as the man's teeth tore through the thick plastic.

Dropping the broken sledge, I backed away. Ameena was beside me, breathing heavily. She didn't look nearly as amused as she had done a minute ago.

'Man,' she muttered, 'I hate zombies.'

'I call them... screechers,' I told her. We were out of the aisle now, moving backwards towards the door. The man on the floor was crawling after us, dragging his injured leg behind him.

'Why?'

As if just waiting for his cue, the man threw back his head and let out an ear-splitting screech.

Ameena looked at me. 'Forget I asked. I think we should run. D'you think we should run?'

I nodded. 'I think we should run.'

And with that agreement reached, we ran.

A thick fog was closing in around us as we dashed through the snow in the vague direction of the police station. We were taking another route back to meet up with Billy and Guggs – one that didn't put us too near the crashed cars, or the alleyways where I'd shaken off the other screechers.

'I still say we should've taken the sledge,' Ameena said, for the third time since we'd left the shop.

'It would've just slowed us down,' I said.

'There was Battenberg cake on that sledge, Kyle. *Battenberg cake.*'

'Well, I'd rather *not* have Battenberg cake and still be alive, wouldn't you?'

It took Ameena a few seconds to answer. 'Can I get back to you on that one?'

A scream came at us through the fog and we both slid to a stop. The sound had been a proper scream, not a screech or a roar or a howl. It had been human – *normal* human – and it had come from somewhere nearby.

'Hear that?' I asked.

'Have to be deaf not to,' Ameena nodded. 'Any idea where it came from?'

We heard the scream again, but this time there were words along with it. 'Help me! Someone help me, please!'

'This way,' I urged, continuing along the road we'd been running along. This time, I made sure I could hear Ameena's footsteps behind me. I wasn't going to lose her again.

'Help! Someone... please, *help*!'

'Someone's in trouble,' I said, racing in the direction of the screams.

'Seriously? You think?' she asked, the sarcasm obvious in her voice. 'What gave that away?'

The voice screamed again, more panicked than ever. 'No, no, please, no!'

KA-RUNCH!

Something large came rolling at us through the fog. Ameena and I threw ourselves in different directions. A dark blue car flipped through the gap between us. It bounced once more on the snowy ground, rolled again, then came to a stop on its roof.

A movement in the back of the car caught my eye. A girl hung there, upside down, struggling with the strap of her seatbelt. Her long blonde hair dangled down, brushing against the inside roof of the car.

She saw me watching her and her eyes opened wide. The windows of the car had all been smashed. Even from this far away, I could hear her gasp with surprise.

'Help me,' she sobbed. 'Get me out. Before it comes back. Help me, *please.*'

Ameena and I scrambled through the snow on our hands and knees until we reached the car. 'Before what comes back?' Ameena asked. 'What did this?'

'Questions later,' I hissed. 'Let's get her out.'

I tried the doors, but their metal frames were buckled and they refused to open. 'It'll have to be the window,' I said.

'Hurry, please,' the girl wept. '*Hurry!*'

'One second,' I promised. Lying down on my back, I reached inside the car and stretched my arm up until I found the seatbelt release button. The buckle was clipped in tight. I pressed the button in a few times, but the belt refused to release.

If you go down to the woods today, you'd better not go alone...

The car's radio hissed into life without warning, making me jump. 'Not again! *Shut up,*' I growled, but the crackly voice of the man on the radio didn't listen.

It's lovely down in the woods today, but safer to stay at home...

'Get me out, please,' begged the girl.

'I'm doing my best,' I said through gritted teeth. I jabbed my thumb on to the button again. Still the seatbelt held. 'God,' I growled. 'I *hate* that song!'

'What song? What are you talking about?'

'You might want to hurry up,' Ameena said from outside the car. 'I can hear something moving out here.'

For every bear that ever there was, will gather there for certain because...

'*That* song,' I hissed. 'Can't you... can't you hear it?'

'No! What are you—'

CLICK!

'Got it!' I cried, just before the girl came thudding, head first, down on top of me. I wriggled free from inside the car, missing out on any more of *The Teddy Bears' Picnic*.

Clambering back to my feet, I reached in through the broken window and helped the girl climb out. The skin of her hand felt soft as I pulled her free of the wreckage. The skin of her face felt even softer when she threw her arms around me and pressed her cheek to mine.

'Thank you,' she sobbed. 'Thank you, you saved me.'

'Um, no one's saved anyone yet.' Ameena's voice was an urgent whisper. The girl and I both followed her gaze until we saw, through the fog, a large, hulking shape. The mist made it difficult to make out any details, although that was probably a blessing.

From what I could tell, our earlier estimate had been right – the thing was about the size of a large rhinoceros. It moved on all fours, its broad head held low to the ground as it stalked slowly in our direction. Its tree-trunk legs sunk into the snow with every step, making it snuffle and snort with frustration.

From the top of my head to the base of my neck began tingling with electricity as my powers sensed they were about to be put to use. I did my best to ignore the sensation. I'd told my dad I wasn't going to use them again, and I had meant every word.

Ameena and I ducked down behind the upturned car. The girl didn't move at first, and I had to catch her by the arm and drag her into hiding alongside us.

'It's coming for me,' she whispered. She was about my height, but a few years older than me, I guessed. The make-up she wore around her eyes was smudged and streaked by tears, and her white jumper was speckled with blood. 'It's coming for me again.'

'Suggestions?' Ameena muttered. The thing was still advancing, but it was moving slowly, like it didn't know exactly where we were.

'A couple,' I answered. 'Fight, or run. That's all I've got at the minute.'

'All those in favour of running?' Ameena asked. She held up a hand and so did I. The girl crouching between us showed no signs of even having been listening.

'Running it is, then,' I nodded. 'If we get split up, get to the police station. I'll meet you there.'

'Roger that.'

I slipped my hand over the girl's and clasped my fingers

around hers. She gripped me tightly, and I could feel each and every tremble her body made.

'What's your name?' I asked her. She didn't look in my direction, just kept her eyes fixed on the shape in the fog. 'Hey,' I said, giving her hand a squeeze. 'What's your name?'

'R-Rosie,' she whispered.

'OK, Rosie, I need you to keep hold of my hand,' I said. 'We're going to run, OK?'

She shook her head from side to side, panic filling her eyes. 'N-no,' she stammered.

'No?' I frowned. The shape was drawing closer through the mist now. I could make out a rough, yellow-ish hide and a bottom jaw that could probably chomp through solid steel. 'What's wrong with running?'

Rosie's grip tightened in mine. Her other arm caught me by the sleeve, holding me beside her. 'It's too fast,' she said, hoarsely, 'we can't outrun it.'

'We're about to find out,' Ameena said, her voice suddenly loud. The shape in the fog hurled back its massive head and let out a thunderous roar. Lunging forward, it cut a trench through the snow. I caught a glimpse of teeth and of sharp, protruding bone and then the car we were hiding behind was crushed beneath the creature's weight.

'Get to the station,' Ameena barked. 'I'll distract it.'

'*Distract it?* Are you nuts?'

'I've seen the way you run, remember? You need all the head-start you can get. Go, I'll meet you there.'

I hesitated, unable to say any of the things I wanted to say to her. 'Don't do anything stupid,' I managed. 'And don't get killed,' I added. 'Promise me.'

'Cross my heart and hope to.... No wait, that doesn't work, does it?' she said. 'I promise. Now *go!*'

With a final glance at the monster's hazy outline, I tightened my grip on Rosie's hand, and together we raced off into the thickening grey fog.

Chapter Twelve

ROSIE'S STORY

'**O**pen the door! Let us in!'

The glass in the police station's front door fogged beneath my breath. It came in huge gulps, swelling my lungs until they felt like they'd burst. Rosie, the girl we'd rescued, stood beside me, still clinging tightly to my hand.

Inside the police station, nothing moved. I cupped my hands against the glass and peered through. 'Billy?' I called. 'Billy, open up!'

'There's no one here,' Rosie whimpered. 'You said there'd be somebody here.'

'There should be,' I muttered. I had just reached for the radio on my belt when a sudden movement on the other side of the window made me jump. Guggs' face appeared beyond the glass. He looked at us both, eyes narrowed.

'Who's she?' he demanded.

'Let us in, Guggs,' I urged. We hadn't encountered any screechers on the way back, but that didn't mean there weren't any nearby. 'Hurry up.'

Guggs jabbed a finger against the glass, leaving a greasy smudge behind. 'Who's she?' he asked again.

'Rosie,' I sighed. 'Her name's Rosie. She was being attacked and we saved her. Now let us in.'

'Attacked? Is she bit?'

'*No*, she hasn't been bitten,' I cried. Then I turned to Rosie. 'You haven't been bitten, have you?'

She shook her head. 'No.'

'No, she hasn't been bitten,' I said. 'Now hurry up and let us in.'

For a few long moments it looked as if Guggs wasn't going to open the door, but then he shook his head, stepped back, and turned the key. I shoved the door open and let Rosie run inside before me.

Another door at the back of the reception area swung open and Billy entered. He was carrying a police baton, twirling it around and around in his hands. He reacted with surprise when he saw us. 'Who's she?' he asked, nodding towards Rosie.

'That's what I said,' Guggs grunted. He moved to lock the door again, but I stopped him.

'Wait, not yet. Look after her,' I said, releasing Rosie's hand. 'I have to go back out.'

'What, *again*?' Billy asked. 'Why?'

'It was... I think it was that thing we heard. The Beast,' I explained. 'Ameena distracted it so we could get away. I have to go back for her.'

Guggs gave a snort. 'You're going to take on the Beast? You're a bigger idiot than I thought. If that thing's half as bad as it sounds, it's probably already torn her to bits. You might as well accept it.'

Had Guggs not been holding his metal bar, I'd have taken a swing at him. With my abilities I could beat him easily. But my abilities weren't an option any more, and so neither was fighting Guggs. But that didn't mean I was going to let him scare me.

'Lock the door behind me,' I said. 'I'm going to find her.'

I turned in time to see Ameena stepping through the door. 'Find who?' she asked, breathing hard.

'Um... you.'

'Right. Well...' She held her arms out to the side and smiled. '*Ta-daa!*' The smile dropped from her face as she stepped inside. 'Now shut the damn door, Huggs, there're monsters out there.'

'Don't push me, sweetheart,' Guggs growled.

Ameena stopped and fixed him with a frosty glare. 'The door, Huggs. Lock the door.'

'Or what?' Guggs asked. His hand was tight around the metal bar. 'Or *what?*'

Billy cleared his throat. The sudden sound surprised everyone and broke the tension. 'Or we'll be wall-to-wall zombies in here,' he shrugged. 'And none of us wants that. Right?'

Guggs shot his cousin a dirty look, but it was nothing compared to the one he fired in Ameena's direction. He didn't argue any more, though. With a *click* the key turned in the lock.

'How'd you get away?' I asked.

Ameena shrugged. 'Just ran in circles for a bit. That seemed to confuse it. I legged it back here before it could figure out which way I'd gone. It's big, but it isn't smart. A bit like Huggs, here.'

'Come across any screechers?' I asked.

She shook her head. 'Nope.'

'What the hell are screechers?' Guggs asked.

'The people out there,' I said. 'The ones chasing us.'

'They're *zombies*, not screechers,' he insisted. '*Screechers.* What kind of stupid name's that? Why'd you call them *screechers*?'

'Because they screech,' I explained.

It took a moment for Guggs to figure out the connection. 'They screech, so you call them screechers? That's rubbish. Why not call them *face-biters*, then? Or... or...' He racked his brain. '...or *crazy freaks that chase you down and eat you?*'

'Yeah, not exactly catchy, that last one,' Ameena pointed out. 'I say screechers is as good a name as any.'

Rosie hadn't spoken since I'd shoved her into the station. She lingered just inside the doorway, fiddling nervously with her long blonde hair. As she listened to us arguing, her blue eyes flitted anxiously across each of our faces. When they got to me I offered her what I hoped came across as a reassuring smile. She didn't smile back, but then I couldn't really blame her.

'Hi,' I said, taking her hand and shaking it. 'I'm Kyle. We didn't really get a chance to do proper introductions earlier.'

'Rosie,' she said, her cheeks blushing pink.

'Yeah, you said,' I reminded her. I let her have her hand back, then turned to the others. 'This is Ameena. She's my... friend.'

'Howdy,' Ameena nodded. Rosie smiled weakly in reply.

'This is Billy,' I said, moving on. 'He's...' I searched for a way to explain my connection to Billy. 'We go to the same school.'

'Hi, it's really lovely to meet you,' Billy said. He was smiling broadly at the girl, almost tripping over himself in his rush to shake her hand. 'Anything you need, just let me know.'

'Thanks,' Rosie said, blushing again.

'And that's Huggs,' Ameena continued, gesturing to the boy by the door. 'He's a shaved ape we stole from the circus. We're teaching him some basic communication skills.'

'Shut up,' Guggs growled.

Ameena grinned her wrinkled-nose grin. 'See? Well done, Huggs. Extra banana for you tomorrow.'

Guggs muttered below his breath, but otherwise said nothing.

'So, you know who we are,' Ameena said. 'Who are you?'

'Rosie,' the girl said. 'My name's Rosie.'

'We got that bit,' Ameena replied. 'Looking for a bit more. What happened to you out there?'

Rosie's face seemed to crumple. She made a noise that sounded almost like the cry of the screechers, but then it became a series of loud sobs. She buried her face in her hands, as if trying to push back the tears that had started to fall.

'Oh, great. Just great,' Guggs said. He turned from the window and stomped towards the door at the back of the room. 'If anyone needs me, I'll be up on the roof.'

'You take care now, Huggs,' Ameena beamed. She waved enthusiastically after him. 'Missing you already.'

The door slammed shut. From beyond it, we heard Guggs punch the wall.

'You shouldn't wind him up so much,' Billy said. 'He's dangerous.'

Ameena shrugged. 'That's what makes it fun.'

I gently rested a hand on Rosie's shoulder. She didn't flinch or pull away, but her hands didn't move from her face, either. She was no longer making any noise, but from the way her body shook it was clear she was still crying.

'It's OK,' I said. 'You're safe now. You're OK.'

'Watch out,' Ameena told me softly. 'I'll handle this.'

I stepped back, letting Ameena in. I wasn't really sure how you dealt with crying girls, so it was good to have another girl around to handle things sensitively.

'Oi. You. Pull yourself together,' Ameena barked. She bumped her fist against Rosie's shoulder, not hard, but not exactly softly either.

'Ameena!' I gasped.

'What? Well, we don't have time for touchy feely.'

'But we don't know what—'

'No, she's right,' Rosie said. She wiped her tears on the back of her sleeve, rubbing away the last streaks of her make-up. Without it she looked younger – still older than me, but not by much. Despite everything, I couldn't help but notice she was pretty too. No wonder Billy had been so nice to her.

'So?' Ameena asked. 'What happened?'

Rosie cleared her throat and wrapped her arms across herself. Her eyes took on a faraway look as she began to speak. 'We were driving. My mum, my dad and me. Heading up north to visit my dad's sister. She's in hospital... although, I don't suppose that matters now.'

'Skip to the good bits,' Ameena urged.

Rosie blushed. 'Sorry,' she said, her voice wobbling. 'We were just meant to be passing through here. The road was clear, everything was fine, but then, all of a sudden, we were driving through snow and the car kept skidding all over the road.'

'When was this?' I asked.

'I... I don't know, exactly. Half an hour ago, maybe?'

'You drove into the village half an hour ago?' Billy asked, suddenly animated. 'That's great! If you could get in, we can get out.'

I knew there had to be more to Rosie's story. Ignoring Billy, I told her to carry on.

'We were turning a corner and the car slid. It hit another car. We weren't going fast, though, so it was fine. My dad tried to reverse, but the wheels just kept spinning.'

Rosie's face went pale. She shook her head, as if

denying the memory playing out behind her eyes. 'And so... and so... he got out. My dad got out. He got out of the car!'

She fell silent then. We all did.

Eventually, it was down to me to ask the obvious question. 'What happened?'

'He was round the front, pushing. My mum was in the driver's seat, trying to reverse. She was looking out of the back window and I was looking at her and we were laughing about the whole thing, and then... Then my dad was gone. And we weren't laughing any more.'

'Where did he go?' Ameena asked.

Rosie shook her head. Her eyes closed for a moment as she fought back more tears. 'He just... He just disappeared. He was there, he was right there, and then he wasn't. There was nothing there but fog. My mum got out then and shouted. Called his name, over and over. He didn't answer. No one answered.'

She took a deep breath. It came out again as a series of unsteady gasps. 'But something heard her. I saw a shape move in the mist behind her. It was big, but it was fast. So, *so* fast. One second it was there, the next it was gone. And... and so was my mum. I heard her scream. But it didn't last long.'

Ameena gave a low whistle through her teeth. 'Bummer,' she said.

'I didn't know what to do. I just sat there. Just sat there, looking out the window, too scared to move. And then it started attacking the car,' Rosie said. Her voice was less wobbly now, but from the way she was clenching her fists, it was clear she was barely holding herself together. 'All I could do was scream. I screamed and screamed and... and... and that's when you two turned up.'

She threw her arms around my neck and buried her face against my shoulder. 'It would've killed me,' she said, sobbing again. 'It would've killed me like it did my mum and dad!'

'Don't say that,' I soothed. I patted her on the back, because it felt like I should be doing something. 'You don't know that, they might be OK.'

'Chances are pretty slim, though,' Billy said. Ameena

and I both shot him a look. 'Um, I mean, yeah,' he added. 'They're probably fine.'

'No, they're not,' Rosie said. She released her grip on my neck, but took hold of my hand instead. I saw Ameena's gaze go to our interlocked fingers. It didn't move for a long time. 'They're dead. I know they're dead. And with that thing out there, we'll be next.'

'Uh, Kyle, a word?' Ameena said. She took a step towards me and pushed me towards the door Guggs had gone through. The shove broke Rosie's grasp on my hand. As we walked through the door, I heard Billy rush to take my place.

'I'll hold your hand if you want,' he offered.

Rosie sniffed and wiped her eyes. 'Thanks,' she said. 'But I'm fine.'

That was the last I heard before Ameena pulled the door closed behind us. We were standing in the corridor that led to the back door of the station. Just a few weeks ago, Mr Mumbles had chased us along it. It felt like a lifetime ago.

'What's up?' I asked.

'Nothing,' she replied curtly.

'Oh. Right. Why'd you want to talk to me then?'

She shrugged. 'I didn't.'

'Um... yes, you did.'

'I don't like her,' she said, matter-of-factly.

'Rosie?' I asked. 'Why not?'

'Because... she keeps crying all the time.'

I nodded. 'Yeah. But then, she did just watch her family get killed.'

'She didn't *watch* them, don't exaggerate,' Ameena replied, rolling her eyes. 'She barely saw a thing.'

'No, but—'

'And what's with all the hugging and the hand-holding? Why's she so touchy feely?' Ameena demanded. 'There's no need for it. She doesn't even know you. There's no need for it.'

A realisation suddenly hit me. 'Wait,' I said. 'You're... you're *jealous*.'

'Of Goldilocks?' she snorted. 'Please. Don't flatter yourself. I just don't trust her, that's all.'

'Because she cries all the time.'

'Yeah. Exactly. Because she cries all the time.'

I nodded. 'OK. We'll keep an eye on her.' I turned to the door. 'We'd better go back through.'

'Wait.' Ameena's grip was like steel on my arm. 'I need to show you something.'

I turned back to her. Her eyes were wide and worried. 'What is it?' I asked. She didn't say anything, so I asked her again. 'What is it?'

'Earlier on. I... uh... I lied,' she told me, her voice a hushed whisper. 'When you asked if I saw any screechers.'

'Oh. Right,' I said. 'So... you did see some?'

'One,' she replied. 'I saw one.'

'Oh,' I said again. 'Right.'

'He, um, jumped out at me from behind a car.'

My mouth suddenly felt dry. 'You got away, though.'

'Yeah, I got away. I got away,' Ameena said. There was a crack in her voice I'd never heard before. 'Just. But not before he gave me this.'

She slowly and carefully pushed her sleeve up. My chest

went tight, like all the air had been sucked from the room. There, just above Ameena's wrist, was a semi-circular tear in her flesh.

'He bit me,' she said. 'The screecher... he bit me.'

Chapter Thirteen

TAKING STOCK

My whole body felt numb when we walked back through to the reception area. Ameena had rolled her sleeve back down before I could even speak, then pushed past me, mouthing a low, 'Don't tell anyone,' just before she opened the door.

'Aye aye,' Billy said, waggling his eyebrows. 'What you two been up to?'

'Shut up, Billy,' we both said at the same time.

'I was only joking,' he muttered.

A red mist of rage descended over my eyes. I changed direction, mid-step, and stormed over to the front desk where Billy stood. A few weeks ago I wouldn't have dreamed of even looking at Billy without permission. He'd seemed like a giant. A monster.

But I'd met real monsters since then. And Billy didn't even come close.

'Don't joke!' I snarled, pushing him against the desk. 'All right? None of this is funny, Billy. No one's laughing.'

'I know!' he said.

'No, you *don't*! You're acting like this is some sort of game. Racing around in that car, all that "destroy the brain" stuff. It's not a zombie movie, Billy, it's real!' The anger was swelling my chest now. Billy looked smaller than ever.

'Rosie's parents are... missing,' I said, narrowly avoiding saying the word "dead". 'My nan is missing. She's out there somewhere, and I don't know where, and you stand there and—'

'They took my sister.'

The rest of my rant caught in my throat. I looked at Billy, but he didn't look back.

'What?'

'Lily,' he said quietly. 'They took Lily.'

'What?' I said again. 'Who did?'

'The zombies. Screechers. Whatever you call them.' Billy looked at his fingernails, still avoiding my gaze. I could feel Ameena beside me. She'd had more to do with saving Lily from Caddie than I had.

'When?' she asked.

'During the night,' he said. 'My mum and dad went out into town. Down the pub. I was babysitting. Again. They were meeting my uncle, so Guggs came round to the house. Lily hates Guggs, though.'

'I knew I liked that kid,' Ameena said.

'She asked me if I'd stay in her room with her when she went to sleep,' Billy said. His eyes glistened and it took him a moment to carry on. 'I said "no".'

He walked away from us then, past Rosie, who was standing in the middle of the room, looking out of place, and over to the tatty couch that sat in the corner of the reception. He flopped down on to it, as if his legs could no longer hold him up.

'Guggs and me, we played Xbox, and he drank a few beers. I don't know what time I fell asleep, but it was Lily's screaming that woke me up. I jumped up and ran to her room, but they were in the hall and I couldn't... I couldn't...'

Billy finally broke. We could barely hear his next words through the sound of his sobs. 'I left her. Guggs told me to leave her and *I just left her.* I left her there with them... *things.*'

'Oh, God,' Ameena whispered. 'You didn't.'

Billy could only nod. He was hugging his legs now, rocking back and forth, weeping silently.

'You let them take her,' I said. 'You let them.'

'N-no,' Billy cried. 'There were too many of them. They were in the hall. *They were in her room!* What could I have done?'

I didn't even try to hide the contempt in my voice. 'You could have tried.'

For a while, no one spoke, each lost in our own thoughts. It was Rosie who eventually said something.

'What are we going to do?'

Ameena slapped her hand down on the reception desk, making everyone jump. 'We need to take stock,' she said, jumping up and sitting cross-legged on the desktop. 'Try to figure out what's going on. What do we know so far?'

I blew out my cheeks. 'Not a lot.'

'That doesn't help. What *do* we know?' She counted off on her fingers. 'We know there's at least one monster roaming around out there. We know something's happened to the people in the village to turn them into... whatever it is they've been turned into.'

'We know there's snow,' Rosie said, trying to get into the spirit of things.

Ameena rolled her eyes. 'Yes, thank you. Very helpful.'

Rosie smiled, missing the sarcasm completely.

'We know they don't die,' Ameena continued. 'The cop, she should've been dead at least twice, but she wasn't.'

'They're strong too,' I added, remembering the dents in the car boot, and the way the man in the shop had bitten clean through the sledge. 'Freakishly strong.'

'Right. What about practicalities?' Ameena asked. The

rest of us looked at her, blankly. 'Phone lines? Food? Weapons?' she explained. 'Where are we at?'

'Not great,' Billy replied. 'There's a packet of biscuits and some teabags through the back. Phone's still dead, and the only weapon I could find was this.' He held up the baton, then lowered it again.

'Right,' Ameena sighed. 'What kind of biscuits?'

'KitKats.'

She nodded. 'Not bad. Not bad. Pity we're screwed on everything else.' She hopped down from the desk. 'So, what else do we know? How did all those people become... the way they are?'

'They got bit,' Billy said.

Ameena rounded on him. 'Did they? How do you know that?'

He shrugged. 'That's how it works, innit? In films.'

'Yes, but we're not *in* a film, are we?'

'No, but... the policewoman,' I said. Ameena turned to look at me, and I could tell she'd already thought the same thing. 'At my house. She'd been... hurt. And she changed.'

'Like in the films,' Billy nodded. 'Like I said.'

'Shut up, Billy,' I told him as Ameena turned away and touched the sleeve that covered her bite mark.

'What else do we know?' she asked, moving the conversation on.

'We know my dad's involved somehow,' I said.

Ameena spun back to face me. 'He is?'

'What?' Billy frowned. 'I thought you didn't have a dad?'

Ameena shook her head. 'He's not *Jesus*, Billy, of course he's got a dad.' She stepped in closer to me. 'What did he say?'

I shrugged. 'The usual.'

'Well, where is he?' Billy asked, standing up. 'Can he help us?'

'No,' I told him. 'He really can't.'

'That *thing*,' Rosie said. We all turned to look at her. 'What did you call it? The Beast?'

'What about it?' I asked.

'Could it have done something to change everyone?'

She brushed her hair back over her ears and seemed to wilt beneath everyone's gaze. 'I mean, I haven't seen the people you're talking about, but it seems like a big coincidence if they're not connected.'

Ameena used her fingers to perform a drum roll on the reception desk. 'And the award for most obvious statement ever goes to... you! Of *course* they're connected. We just don't know how yet.'

'Well, however they're connected, we can't stay here,' Billy said. 'It's Monster Central out there. How long are we going to last sitting around here?'

'The streets are filled with those things. The routes out of town are blocked. What do you suggest?' Ameena asked, but Billy had no answer to give her.

'I think I remember the route we came in,' Rosie offered. 'If we can get a car, I should be able to get us back on to the main road. There's no snow there.'

Ameena thought about this for a minute. Eventually she turned to me. 'What do you think?'

'I have to stay,' I told her. 'I have to find Nan.'

'Then I'll stay too,' Ameena said. 'But the rest of you should go.'

Billy nodded. 'No complaints from me.'

'We'll send help,' Rosie added. 'When we get to the town.'

'Right. Good,' Ameena said, nodding her head. 'Oh, and – just so we're absolutely clear – *we're* keeping the KitKats.'

'Fair enough,' replied Billy. 'Now all we have to do is find a car.'

'There's a little car park out the back,' Ameena told him. 'There's usually a cop car there.'

'How do you know that?'

Ameena glanced at me, then back to Billy. 'Long story.'

'So, is it decided then?' I asked. 'Me and Ameena will stay. Billy – you, Rosie and Guggs will try to get out of the village. Rosie, stick with Billy. He'll look after you. Probably.'

'And watch out for Huggs,' Ameena added. 'He's a groper.'

'I'd better go get him,' Billy said. He sounded reluctant. It was clear that he disliked his cousin almost as much as everyone else did. He started to walk towards the door, but it opened before he was halfway there. Guggs strode through it, sounding out of breath.

'Billy,' he said, hurrying over to the front doors. He looked through the glass at the street outside. 'Check it out.'

Billy joined him at the window. Curiosity got the better of me and I followed on behind. Ameena and Rosie came over too, and soon we were all lined up, peering out through the glass.

In the time since we'd come back to the police station, the daylight had begun to fade. What was left of it reflected off the snow, making the ground look like it was faintly glowing.

'What am I looking at?' Billy asked.

'Wait for it,' Guggs muttered. He was looking along the street, to where the corner of a neighbouring building blocked the rest of the road from view. 'The fog's lifted.

You can see the whole street from the roof,' he explained. 'I was looking that way when— There, look!'

Billy made a sound that was halfway between a sob and a cheer. He stared – we all did – as a little girl in pink pyjamas trudged determinedly through the snow.

'Lily,' he whispered. 'It's her. It's Lily. She's still alive!'

Chapter Fourteen

LILY THE PINK

Billy banged his fists against the door. 'Lily!' he cried. 'Lily, over here!'

Outside, his sister did nothing to indicate she had heard him. Billy scrambled for the key that would unlock the doors. He'd just got a hand to it when Guggs grabbed him and pulled him back.

'What are you doing?' Guggs demanded. 'Have you gone nuts?'

Billy shook his head. 'It's Lily, Guggs. It's Lily, she's all right!'

'You don't know that,' his cousin spat. 'For all we know she's one of them.'

'No, she isn't. She's... she's just Lily!' Billy grabbed for the key a second time. 'I have to get her. I'm not leaving her again.'

Guggs caught him by the arms and held on to him. 'It's too late,' he snarled. 'It's too dangerous. You're not going out there. No one's going out there.'

Click. Rosie turned the key in the lock. 'She's... um... she's his sister,' she said, too scared to meet Guggs' glare. 'It, uh, it should be his decision.'

Ameena nudged me in the ribs. 'D'you know,' she said, loudly enough for everyone to hear, 'I'm really starting to warm to that girl?'

Billy lunged for the door, but this time it was me who stopped him. 'Hold on,' I warned him. 'I hate to say it, but Guggs is right. It's dangerous out there.'

Yanking his arm away, Billy looked at me in horror. 'I'm not leaving her alone. Not again.'

'Of course not,' I said. 'But let's be careful. I'll come and watch your back.'

'And I'll come and watch yours,' Ameena told me.

Rosie moved closer to me. 'I'm not staying in here with him,' she said, glancing briefly at Guggs.

'You'll be safer in here,' I said.

'It's fine,' said Ameena, 'I'll watch her.'

'Right. OK. Is that it? Can I go and get my sister now?' Billy snapped.

I gave a nod and he swung the door open. The snow crunched beneath our feet as we stepped on to the pavement.

'Hang back here,' I whispered to Ameena. 'Keep your eyes open.'

'Roger that,' she nodded. Keeping Rosie beside her, she took up position just outside the door and began scanning for danger.

Lily was still trudging slowly along the street. The snow was almost to her waist, and we could see a long, straight trench showing the route she had walked to get here.

'Don't shout to her,' I warned, stopping Billy just as he opened his mouth. 'You'll attract attention. Let's just go and get her.'

Billy didn't wait to be told twice. He hurried forwards, stumbling through the blanket of white on the ground. I stuck close behind him, keeping one eye on Lily, and one on the streets around us. The mist had mostly lifted, but now the darkening sky made it difficult to see.

We closed the gap between the station and Lily in less than twenty seconds. Billy slowed when we got close to her. She was walking away from the station now, and we'd approached her from behind.

Softly, Billy cleared his throat and spoke her name. 'Lily?'

The girl in the pink pyjamas stopped.

'Lily,' he said again. 'It's me. It's Billy. It's... it's Bro-Bro.'

There was no reaction from his sister. I looked at her frail back, covered only by a thin pyjama top. She was half-buried in snow. Presumably her feet were bare. And yet, she wasn't shivering.

'Billy, wait,' I said, as he reached a hand out towards her. There was no stopping him, though. His big hand clamped down on her narrow shoulder, and at that, she turned around.

Her eyes were like two black holes in her face. Her little head twitched like a bird's as she looked from Billy to me and back again.

'Aw, no,' Billy croaked. His hand was still on Lily's shoulder. I pulled him back, putting some distance between them. 'Aw, no, not Lily,' he whimpered. 'Not her.'

Lily's bottom jaw dropped open. Clouds of white breath rolled from her mouth as she threw back her head and let out an ear-splitting cry. All around us, other voices screeched in reply.

'Kyle!' Ameena's shout was high-pitched with panic. I whipped around and saw dozens of figures come running from the darkness on all sides, crashing and hurdling through the snow towards us.

'Inside!' I bellowed, already dragging Billy back towards the station. 'Get inside, now!'

Ameena shoved the door. From fifteen metres away, I

heard her gasp. 'Locked it. He's locked it!' She hammered her clenched fists against the glass. 'Open the door,' she screamed. 'Open the damn door!'

Billy and I reached the door at the same time. Guggs stood beyond the glass, grinning out at us. Behind us, the screechers closed the gap. Lily hadn't moved, but the others were now only twenty or thirty seconds away.

'Guggs, open the door!' I said. 'Come on!'

'What, so you and your infected girlfriend can get back in? Not likely.'

He saw the surprise on my face. 'I heard you when you were in the corridor,' he said. He pointed at Ameena, right between the eyes. 'You got bit.'

'They're getting closer,' Rosie wailed.

'Come on, cuz, open up,' Billy begged. 'Please.'

'Self-preservation, Bill,' Guggs shrugged. 'I told you not to go outside.'

Rosie grabbed me by the sleeve. 'They're coming!'

'Smash the glass!' Billy yelped.

'What's the point? Then they can follow us in,' Ameena said.

I was about to try to reason with Guggs again, when I saw something move in the doorway behind him. 'Billy,' I said quietly. 'When you got here, you checked all the rooms, right?'

'Most of them, yeah. Why?'

'*Most* of them?'

The shape in the doorway became a man. He wore a police uniform and his eyes were as black as coal.

'Guggs, look out!' I warned, but the screecher was too fast. He bounded across the room in three big leaps. I saw his jaw unhinge, heard Guggs scream, and then a spray of dark blood covered the glass.

Screams of rage were suddenly all around us. I turned, just as a screecher launched herself towards me. Twisting and ducking, I got out of her path. She hit the glass with a hollow *thonk*, landed on all fours, then turned to face me once again.

'Split up,' I yelped, as more of the screechers reached us.

'Meet at the Keller House,' I added, remembering the wooden boards nailed across most of the house's windows and doors. 'Rosie, go with Billy!'

I dodged another screecher, avoided his grip, escaped the gnashing of his terrible teeth. I saw another one throw itself at Ameena. Her boot connected with his chin, snapping his head back. She moved to follow me, but more of the infected blocked her path.

'Go,' she barked. 'The Keller House. I'll be there.'

The snow was churning up around us, as more and more screechers arrived at the scene. The air was filled with their squeals and cries. It took everything I had not to collapse into tears.

'Promise?' I asked.

She nodded. 'Promise.'

Billy and Rosie were already running, screechers at their backs. 'Come on, then!' I bellowed, waving my hands in the air. 'Come and get me.'

I turned tail and fled then, still shouting at the screechers, trying to draw them after me and away from Ameena. The plan worked better than I expected. Ten or more of them came after me, sprinting or bounding on all fours through the snow.

I ran along the street. Up ahead I spotted the church, with its heavy wooden doors. Immediately, I wished I'd told everyone to meet there instead of the Keller House. Still, it might prove handy yet.

The screechers were close behind me as I two-at-a-timed up the church steps. The D-shaped metal handles on the doors were freezing to the touch when I grabbed hold of them. I turned them both. The door on the left stayed closed, but the one on the right swung open.

Throwing myself inside, I rushed to slam the door shut behind me. But an arm made it through the gap before I could get it closed. I heard the damp *crack* of snapping bone and the screecher outside howled with rage.

The weight of the door became too much and I was sent stumbling backwards into the church. Screechers rushed in, but I was already heading for the swing doors that led from the foyer into the main bit of the church.

My footsteps clattered along the polished aisle. They echoed around me as I passed beneath the towering statue of Jesus on the cross and barged my way through to the back rooms. More footsteps thudded through the church, faster and faster, gaining on me with every step.

I stumbled into a small, draughty hall. It stank of damp and of cold, like the attic at home. A door stood at the end of the hall, leading out to the graveyard at the back of the church. I raced towards it and found it unlocked. Shoving the door open, I hurried back outside. It closed with a *bang* just as the screechers entered the hall.

A second later, the first of them hurled itself against the door. The door shook in its frame, but it held fast. Sooner or later, though, it would give way. Either that, or they'd figure out how to use a door handle. Whatever, I couldn't stand around there for long.

The graveyard was as still and silent as... well, as the

grave. The snow had piled up in drifts around the crumbling headstones. I had to go slowly to avoid tripping up on the hidden slabs.

The screechers were still hammering on the door when I finally reached the back fence. I squeezed myself through the gap left by a missing bar and emerged on to Wilkinson Road. From here, I was only two streets and the hill away from my house. From my house, I was only a few dozen metres to the Keller House and, I hoped, to Ameena and the others.

The journey there was straightforward enough. I skirted along at the edges of the streets, in the shadows of garden fences and walls, until I reached my house. The police car was still out front, but its lights were off, the battery presumably having long since gone dead.

I couldn't help but look in the window as I passed my house. I don't know what I hoped to see. Nan, maybe, sitting in her favourite chair. Or Mum, watching TV, like none of this stuff had ever actually happened.

But the armchair was empty. The room was empty. As I'd known it would be.

I cleared the fence between my garden and the Keller House's. The house itself loomed before me, dark and foreboding. I did not like this house. I did not want to be near this house, but right now, it was probably the safest place for miles around. Even knowing that, though, I felt a shiver of fear pass through me as I made for the front door.

I'd used my abilities to tear the boards away earlier, but the door itself was still intact. It was standing open, just as we'd left it. That meant two things. It meant I'd got here before Ameena, Billy or Rosie. And it meant that *anything* could've found its way inside.

Steadying my nerves, I inched the door closed and the room was flooded with absolute blackness. I stayed by the doorway, my hand still on the handle, waiting for my eyes to adjust to the absence of light.

Unable to see, my other senses worked harder to

compensate. That's the only reason I heard it. The only reason that I heard the breathing.

It was close behind me, little more than a few centimetres away. I was about to open the door again and make a run for it, when a man's voice sounded in the near-silence.

'Blimey,' he said. 'Isn't it dark?'

Chapter Fifteen

A MOMENT LIKE THIS

A battery-operated lamp flickered on, bathing the room in a stark white light. I blinked in the sudden glare.

'Oh, sorry,' said the man standing across from me. 'Probably should've warned you I was about to do that.'

'Joseph,' I said, surprised to see him here. Of all the things that had happened to me recently, Joseph was probably the most mysterious. He had cropped up in all kinds of places over the past few weeks – dressed as a policeman in the police station on the day Mr Mumbles had returned, hiding behind the curtain in my school canteen, disguised as a ticket collector on a train I was on. He'd even left a message for me in the Darkest Corners, showing me how to find the cure I needed to get back home.

Although it hadn't always been obvious, he'd been helping me the whole way through. But I still didn't really know who he was.

'What are you doing here?' I asked him.

He rocked on his heels and smoothed out his thick moustache. The glow of the lamp reflected off his balding head. 'Why wouldn't I be?' he asked, gesturing around at the peeling wallpaper and the tatty furniture. 'It's my house, after all.'

I frowned. 'No it isn't,' I said. 'It's Mr Keller's house.'

Mr Keller was an old neighbour who had once saved me from drowning in his swimming pool. I'd been five years old and had just discovered Mr Mumbles' dark side for the first time. Technically, I'd been dead, but Mr Keller had dragged me out of the water and performed CPR until I wasn't dead any more. He'd walked out of his house the next day, and had never returned.

Until now.

'You... You're him,' I realised. 'You're Mr Keller.'

Joseph smiled. 'And at last the penny drops. Yes, that's right. I'm Mr Keller.'

'But... I don't... Why didn't you tell me?' I asked, still taking it all in.

'You didn't ask.'

I held my hands out, palm upwards. 'Well, why would I?' I said. 'I don't go round randomly asking people if they're my old next door neighbour.'

He shrugged. 'Well, if you had done, I'd have said "yes". I did tell you I go by lots of names.'

'Yes, but you didn't tell me Mr Keller was one of them.'

'I guess I thought maybe you'd recognise me,' he said. 'Although I suppose I had more hair back in them days. Or was it less?' He shook his head. 'I lose track.'

'You were in the Darkest Corners,' I said. 'You left me clues. How?'

'I just wrote them on the skirting board in pencil,' he explained. 'It wasn't difficult.'

'I meant, how did you get there? What were you doing in the Darkest Corners?'

His eyes sparkled with mischief. 'Leaving clues for you,' he said.

'Look, can we drop the mystery man act?' I snapped. 'I'm *really* not in the mood. Why can't you just give me straight answers for once?'

Joseph walked over to a floral-patterned armchair and sat down in it. He brushed some dust off the arms, then turned back to me. 'Honestly? I'm worried I might give too much away.'

'No, that'd be a good thing,' I said. 'Give too much away. Give everything away. Whatever you know, *tell me*!'

He smiled, but there were pools of sadness in his eyes. 'I wish I could,' he said. 'But I can't risk changing anything.'

'What?' I asked. '"Changing anything"? What's that supposed to mean?'

He looked at me in silence for a long time. Then, just as I was about to say something, he beat me to it. 'I see the future.'

Normally, I'd have laughed, but the way he said it, and all the things I'd seen in the past few weeks made me pay attention. 'The future?' I said.

'Not all of it,' he replied, standing up. 'Just flashes, really. Moments in time. That's how I've known where to find you, and how I knew where to hide the cure in the hospital. I'd seen those moments before. All of them.'

'What else have you seen?' I asked.

He gave his head a shake. 'Sorry, I can't tell you that. If I tell you, you might do something differently, and that would change everything.'

'Good!' I cried. 'I want everything to change!'

'You don't know that, Kyle,' Joseph replied. 'You don't know what's going to happen.'

'Well tell me then. Tell me what's going to happen.'

'I'm afraid it doesn't work like that. I can't tell you. You have to find out for yourself.'

'At least tell me about Nan,' I demanded. 'Do I find her?'

'I can't. I'm sorry.'

'Come on, Joseph. *Please*,' I begged. 'Just tell me if I find her. Please.'

Joseph looked down at the swirly-patterned carpet at his feet. He gave a deep sigh, then met my gaze again. 'Yes,' he said. 'You find her.'

'I do? Well, that's... Is she alive?'

'Look, this really isn't a good idea,' he began, but I cut him off before he could go any further.

'Please, Joseph. When I find her, is she alive?'

He gave a single nod of his head. 'Yes,' he said. 'She is.'

Everything inside me suddenly felt light. Despite everything, I wanted to leap into the air and cheer. Nan was OK. She was OK!

'When?' I asked. 'When do I find her?'

'Soon,' he said quietly. 'Not long now.'

'Well, where is she?' I asked. I was babbling now, excited at the prospect of finding Nan. 'Is she close by?'

'Closer than you realise,' Joseph replied. He pulled on a grey suit jacket, and I realised for the first time that he was wearing a shirt and tie. 'But I've already said too much.'

'You can't go yet,' I told him. 'It's too dangerous. And I need your help.'

He began to button up the jacket. 'You'll figure it out, Kyle. You always do. You're becoming quite the hero, if I do say so myself.'

'What about my mum?' I asked, trying to get as much information from him as possible before he did his usual disappearing trick. 'Will she be OK?'

'Again, I can't tell you that,' he said. 'And anyway, even I don't have all the answers. I don't know everything that's going to happen. I just know what's going to happen at certain moments. Moments like when we met in the police station, and at your school.' He cleared his throat, and for the first time ever he sounded afraid. 'And moments like this one. Moments like now.'

He walked over to the window. The glass was still in the pane, but a wooden board covered it from the outside. Joseph ran his fingers over the glass, then turned his back on it. He adjusted his tie, then looked over at me.

'I don't know everything that's going to happen,' he repeated. 'But I know, if you're going to have any chance of winning and doing what you need to do, the things I *have* seen need to play out exactly as I saw them. No matter what the cost might be.'

'Doing what I need to do? What do I need to do?'

He smiled at me shakily. 'Save the world.'

I took a step towards him. 'What? What do you mean?'

'Stay there, Kyle,' he said. 'Don't come any closer.'

I stopped walking, but kept staring at him, waiting for an answer. 'What do you mean?'

'The only way I can know you're going to save everyone, is if everything I saw happens *exactly* the way I saw it. It's my job to make *sure* it happens the way I saw it. I daren't change anything, or who knows what the cost might be?'

'Change anything? Like what? I don't understand,' I told him.

'You're a fine boy, Kyle,' he said. He had a watch in the pocket of his jacket. He took it out, looked at it, then put it away again. His voice suddenly sounded raw with emotion. 'One day, I hope, you'll be thought of as a fine man.'

'Um... thanks, but—'

'Goodbye, Kyle,' he said. He touched his forehead just above his right eyebrow and fired off an informal salute. 'And good luck.'

Before I could ask him anything else, something tore through the wooden board that covered the window. I ducked and stumbled back as the room was filled with flying fragments of shattered glass.

A monstrous shape, all teeth and claws and wide, flared nostrils filled the broken window frame. Joseph closed his eyes. A split-second later, a long, bone-like spike burst through his chest, and then he was gone, dragged out into the darkness by the Beast.

My abilities flared. I felt the electrical tingle across my skin as I rushed to the hole in the wall and looked out into the gloom.

A spray of blood covered the snow just outside the house, but that was the only clue that anything had happened here. The darkening night was quiet, and neither Joseph nor the Beast were anywhere in sight.

Chapter Sixteen

SURROUNDED

I was slumped on the floor ten minutes later when the door opened and Ameena stepped through. Other footsteps hurried into the house behind her. Billy and Rosie. All three of them were safe. In my head, I knew this was good news, but the hollowness in my chest wouldn't let me feel relief, or happiness, or anything else for that matter.

He had known what was coming. He had known what was going to happen to him, and he had *let* it happen. And why? So he didn't mess things up for me. So he didn't ruin my chances of "winning", as he put it.

He had died. He had died protecting me. And I didn't even know who he really was.

'Hi honey, we're home,' Ameena said, closing the front door. She looked down at me, slumped on the carpet. 'Don't get too excited, will you?'

'Sorry,' I said, doing my best to hide the tremble in my voice, 'I'm glad you're OK.'

Her eyes narrowed. 'What happened?' she asked.

I swallowed, fighting back tears. 'I... I don't know,' I admitted. 'I mean... I just don't know.'

'I thought this place was supposed to be barricaded?' Billy asked. 'That window's broken. The screechers can get in.'

'He's right,' Ameena nodded. 'What happened?'

I shrugged. The broken window felt like one problem too many. I was already dangerously close to breaking point. If something else came up, there was a good chance I'd lose the plot completely.

'Right, then,' Ameena said. She pointed to a door that led off from the living room. 'Stairs are that way. Billy, take Goldilocks and wait up there. We'll be up in a minute.'

'Don't be long,' Billy said below his breath. 'Rosie's scared.'

'Yeah. *Rosie's* scared,' Ameena snorted. 'Relax, Billy, we'll be up to look after you in a minute.'

Without saying any more, Billy led Rosie out through the door. We listened to the creaking of their footsteps on the stairs until they made it all the way to the top.

Ameena sat down on the floor beside me. She ducked her head, trying to meet my eye, but I didn't look up. 'So,' she began. 'What's up?'

'Joseph's dead.'

From the corner of my eye I saw the shock cross her face. 'What? How? When?'

'Few minutes ago,' I said. 'He was... He was standing there at the window and the Beast came through. It took him.'

'Good grief,' Ameena muttered. She looked at the window, as if trying to imagine the scene I'd witnessed. 'And are you sure he's dead?'

I remembered the bony spike through Joseph's chest. 'Pretty sure.'

Ameena fell silent. She looked at the splintered wood and broken glass of the window. 'That's terrible,' she said. 'And I know this is going to sound harsh, what with the poor guy having just been killed, but did he tell you anything useful?'

'Not really,' I said, after a pause. I decided not to tell her about the Mr Keller connection. Not at the moment, anyway. She'd ask too many questions, and I didn't feel like answering any right at that moment. In fact, I didn't feel like doing anything. 'I'm sick of this,' I told her.

She didn't reply, just gave me a sympathetic smile.

'I'm sick of running all the time. Sick of everyone getting hurt, or worse. I wish... I wish it would all just end.'

'It can, if you like,' Ameena shrugged. 'You can step outside and wait for the screechers to get you. Might sting a bit, but it'd be over in no time.'

I thought about this for a moment. 'Nah.'

'No, didn't think so,' Ameena nodded. 'So quit complaining. Superheroes don't complain.'

'I'm not a superhero,' I replied. 'And I can't use my abilities either. Everything the Crowmaster told me was true. Every time I use my power, I'm bringing the world closer to disaster. I'm playing right into my dad's hands.'

'Ah. Right. That's... a shame,' Ameena sighed. 'That's going to hamper the monster fighting a bit.'

'A bit, yeah. How's your arm?' I asked her.

Her body language became defensive. 'Fine,' she said. 'Kind of hurts, but that's no surprise.'

I looked at her for the first time since she'd sat down. 'Any... side effects?'

She shook her head. 'Nope. Right as rain. I guess getting bitten doesn't change you, after all.'

'That's a relief,' I said.

'Yeah, although it won't do you much good if they're eating you alive.'

'Fair point,' I conceded. 'If it isn't the bites, then, what is it? What's changing people?'

Ameena shrugged. 'No idea.'

'Well, I'm glad you're OK,' I said. 'I'm not sure I could have handled it if you'd... changed.'

'Doubt I'd have enjoyed it much either,' she said. 'Still, at least you'd have Goldilocks. She didn't stop talking about you the whole way back. She's into you in a big way.'

'Really?' I asked, my eyebrows raised.

'*Big* way,' Ameena nodded.

I thought about this for a second, but couldn't quite get it to make sense in my head. 'Why would she like *me*?'

Ameena opened her mouth to say something, then thought better of it and closed it again. She smiled, but it wasn't her usual cocky grin. 'Beats me,' she said.

Pieces of glass crunched beneath her boots as she stood up. She held a hand out to me. I took it without hesitation. 'Come on,' she said, hauling me to my feet, 'we'd better get upstairs before those two start wetting their pants.'

'What about the window?' I asked. 'Should we barricade it again?'

Ameena glanced at the hole. 'Too tricky. It'll be easier to block the stairs.'

'Right. And then what?'

She looked upwards for a moment, deep in thought. 'We'll think of something,' was all she came up with. 'Let's go.'

'So, what do we do?'

Billy was sitting on the floor in the empty box room, his back propped against a damp-stained wall. I sat on the windowsill, my body angled so I could easily see outside. The lights were still burning inside my house. The streak of red that had been outside the back door was now gone, completely covered by the snow.

As soon as we'd entered the room, Rosie had run over and thrown her arms around me. Her skin felt warm against mine. She smelled *amazing*. There was nothing I could do to stop myself returning the hug.

When we finally let go, Ameena was looking the other way, facing the bedroom door. It was several minutes before she looked in my direction again.

'Hello? Anyone?' Billy said. 'What do we do?'

'I don't know, Billy,' I sighed. 'I don't know what to do.'

Billy stood up.

'Right, fine then,' he said with a scowl. 'If you're not going to take charge, then *I* am.'

'Sit down, Billy,' said Ameena sternly.

Billy sat down.

'Well, we can't just sit around here waiting to die,' he mumbled. 'We've got to do *something*.'

'You're right. We do,' I nodded. 'We're going to stick to the original plan. You and Rosie are going to get out of the village.' I turned to Ameena, knowing full well she wasn't going to like what I was about to say. 'And I want you to go with them.'

Ameena snorted. 'Yeah, like that's going to happen. I'm staying with you.'

'No,' I told her, pulling her aside. 'You aren't. You're a good friend,' I said. 'You're... you're the best friend I've ever had, Ameena. And I want you to keep being my friend for a long time.'

'Shut up,' she said. *Was she blushing?*

'And for that, you have to be alive.'

'Yeah, well so do you,' she retorted, 'and there's no way you're going to avoid being killed by yourself.'

'A few weeks ago, maybe,' I agreed, 'but I've been to the Darkest Corners and I made it back. I survived – I even saved someone else – and I did it on my own.'

Her eyebrows knotted. 'So, what you saying? You don't need me any more? Is that it?'

'No, just the opposite,' I said. 'It's because I *do* need you that I want you to go. I can't let anything happen to you. Not you too.'

I searched her face, trying to gauge her reaction. I

needn't have bothered. 'Tough,' she said firmly. 'I'm staying.'

'Ameena, listen to me,' I pleaded, but a whisper from Rosie stopped me short. She was standing by the window, keeping look-out.

'Uh, everyone?' she said. 'You might want to come and see this.'

We gathered around the window, all four of us, and looked down at the garden below. I realised, in that moment, that arguing with Ameena was pointless. She wasn't getting out of the village. And nor was anyone else.

'This is your fault,' Billy spat, shooting me an evil look. 'If you hadn't wasted time talking to your girlfriend we could've been out of here. We could've been safe.'

'Are... are you his girlfriend?' Rosie asked. Ameena blanked her and turned to Billy instead. Outside, half-hidden by the dusk, an army of screechers swarmed towards the house.

'Shut up, Billy,' she warned. 'This is no one's fault.'

233

'What are you even doing here, anyway?' Billy demanded. 'You've been bit. You're one of *them*!'

'Does she look like one of them?' I snapped. 'Really?'

'Not yet, but it's only a matter of time!'

'No, it isn't, Billy,' I said. 'Look, she's fine. There's nothing wrong with her. Now shut up so I can figure out what we do next.'

'What we do next?' he spluttered. He gestured down to the garden. More screechers were climbing or leaping over the fence, headed in our direction. 'What we do next is *die*, Kyle. Can't you see that?' He looked me up and down. 'Unless you're going to do your... whatever it is you do.'

I shook my head. 'I can't,' I said.

'You might have to,' Ameena said softly. 'If there's no other way.'

'But... I can't,' I said. 'Something terrible might happen.'

'Something terrible will *definitely* happen if you don't,' she pointed out. 'Involving their teeth and our innards!'

There was a *crash* from downstairs, then a screech from directly below us. 'They're in the house,' Rosie whimpered. 'They're already in the house. What do we do?'

'It's OK,' Ameena said. 'We closed the door to the stairs and jammed it with a chair. They can't get up. We've got time.'

Rosie's bottom lip trembled, but she held herself together. 'Time for what?'

Ameena rubbed her temples, as if trying to ease a headache. 'I Spy?' she suggested. Despite the danger we were in, I almost smiled at that.

'Time to try to figure out exactly what's happening,' I said. 'If we can do that, maybe we can find a way to stop it.'

'We know what's happening,' Billy grunted. 'There's a big monster and lots of zombies. What's to figure out?'

'But where did they come from?' I asked. 'Not from biting each other, or Ameena would be one already. So where?'

'I don't know! Maybe... maybe she's immune somehow?'

My eyes met Ameena's. 'That's a possibility,' I admitted. 'You sure you feel OK?'

'Fine,' she said promptly. 'No change.'

THUD! The screechers hit the door hard. Even up here, we felt the floor shake. A quick glance outside told me they were still coming. The garden was filled with them now, and the night was filled with their cries. They raced across the snow-covered lawn and flung themselves against the house's walls. Although some had clearly found their way inside, most of them weren't smart enough to have discovered a way in.

'OK, so what do we do now?' I asked. Something *thumped* against the floor beneath our feet. 'The screechers. How do we stop them?'

Billy jumped in first. 'Destroy the brain.'

'We're not destroying anyone's brain,' I reminded him. 'They're people, Billy.'

'They *were* people, you mean.'

'So, what about Lily?' I barked. 'Huh? You going to bash her head in too? You going to destroy *her* brain?'

Ameena stepped between us. 'Taking out their legs seems to work,' she suggested. 'Sends them to the floor, but doesn't kill them.'

It sounded like an out of control party was going on downstairs now. Dozens of sets of feet trampled through the rooms below. Screeches and screams and high-pitched howls rose up through the box-room floor. Any minute now I half-expected to hear someone start singing karaoke.

'They're going to get in, aren't they?' Rosie said. Her voice was flat, almost emotionless, as if she had already accepted her fate.

I nodded. There was no point lying. Not any more. 'Yes. They are.'

There was silence in the room then, aside from the sounds of the screechers outside and below. I gawped with surprise as Rosie kissed me lightly on the cheek. 'Thanks for trying,' she said, and as she did her eyes became misty with tears. 'You saved me once already today. But maybe it's just my day to die.'

A tingle crept down my spine and out to the tips of my fingers. I felt my muscles tighten and my hands ball into fists. 'No,' I said. 'No one else is dying because of me.'

I crossed to the window. Back when we'd fought Mr Mumbles, Ameena and I had climbed up on to the roof of this very house. I doubted the screechers could follow us up there. Door handles, after all, seemed to be enough to outwit them, never mind drainpipes. We'd still be trapped up there on the roof, but we'd at least be relatively safe.

'OK,' I began. 'I've got an idea. We're going to—'

KA-RAAASH!

The window exploded inwards, spraying glass in my face. A snarling shape slammed into my chest and I hit the floor just as Rosie began screaming. Black eyes and chomping teeth filled my field of vision. Something sharp slashed across my belly, making me hiss with pain.

I scrabbled backwards, kicking out. The monster squatted on all fours in the middle of the room, spitting and seething as it sized us up.

The monster with the dark eyes, sandpaper skin and impossibly large jaws.

The monster with the sharp, elongated bones jutting from every one of its muscular limbs.

The monster – I realised to my horror – in the police uniform.

Chapter Seventeen

FACING THE BEAST

Blade-like bones stabbed through the back of the uniform, each one several centimetres long. Other bones grew from the monster's cheeks. They curved upwards until they met its forehead, like protective shields for the creature's eyes.

I thought those words: *Monster. Creature.* But I knew she was neither of those things. It was the policewoman. The policewoman I had watched die in my arms. She was barely recognisable now. If it hadn't been for the uniform, I'd never have realised it was her.

'What is it? What is it?' Billy squirmed. He was flat against the wall, but was still trying to back further away. Rosie had lost the plot. I couldn't blame her. She was screaming and pulling at her own hair, unable to tear her eyes away from the terrifying vision before her.

Drawn by her screams, the policewoman spun around. Her jaw dropped open wide enough to swallow Rosie's entire head in a single bite. A shrill, demonic screech filled the room and the monster pounced.

Lightning flashed through me. Consequences or not, I couldn't just stand by and watch Rosie die!

Luckily, I didn't have to. Ameena's boot crunched into the creature, mid-leap. It was knocked sideways and slammed, head-first, into the wall. Ameena grabbed Rosie's arm and threw her towards the door.

'Move, Billy,' she cried. He came running past me just as I stumbled to my feet. The policewoman twisted, tensed her legs and leapt after us. Ameena pulled me through the doorway, then closed the door with a loud *slam*.

We heard the wood splinter, saw it bulge outward. A serrated spike, like a smaller version of the one that had killed Joseph, stabbed through the door, missing me by a centimetre.

As I watched the bony blade withdraw, I suddenly understood what was going on. 'They're changing,' I realised. 'The screechers. They're all changing.'

'Changing into what?' Billy yelped.

'She... she looked like the Beast,' I realised, picturing the creature's dark eyes and snapping jaws.

Billy scowled. 'Eh?'

'The screechers aren't turning into zombies, they're turning into *Beasts*!'

'They're *baby* Beasts,' Ameena nodded. 'Makes sense. In an oh-my-god-somebody-please-kill-me-now kind of way.'

Another spike ripped through the door, tearing a fist-sized hole in the wood. Rosie opened her mouth to scream again, but Ameena slapped her across the face before she could even start.

'Scream later,' she ordered. 'Run now.'

'Run?' Billy cried. At the bottom of the stairs, the other door gave a loud, worrying *crack*. 'Run *where*?'

Ameena gave me a meaningful look. 'Kyle? We need a way out.'

I hesitated. 'I can't,' I fretted. 'My dad admitted everything. He told me what would happen if I kept using my powers. He told me millions of people would die.'

'Or maybe that's just what he *wants* you to believe. Maybe he really just wants *you* dead! Did you think of that?'

The policewoman gave another screech as her head broke through the door. Her jaws gnashed and gnawed at us as she tried to squeeze her body through the gap.

'Oh, too tempting,' Ameena said. She raised her leg and drove the sole of her boot against the policewoman's deformed face, shoving it back through the hole. 'Now,' she said, turning back to me. 'Get us out of here, or I'll kill you myself.'

I felt Rosie's hand grip mine. 'Please,' she whimpered. 'If you can do something, *please* do it. I don't want to die. Not like this. Not like *this*.'

I looked at their faces in turn. *No one else dies*, that's what I'd said. *No one else dies because of me*.

'OK,' I said shakily. 'I'll do it. Stand back.'

Ameena pulled the other two away, along the upstairs landing, near to where the bathroom door stood half open. Behind me, the policewoman's arm clawed through the gap in the door. At the bottom of the stairs, the other screechers were still trying to force their way through.

I closed my eyes. I didn't want to use my abilities. It felt like a victory for my dad, and that was the last thing I wanted. But what alternative was there? What other choice did I have?

The sparks moved through my brain. I held my breath, ignoring the banging and the screaming that now filled every corner of the house, and I focused. I felt my powers surge, then a noise like an explosion drowned out every other sound.

I staggered into the wall as the whole building gave a sudden lurch sideways. The floor became a steep hill. Rosie screamed again as she and the others came tumbling towards me.

'What did you do?' Ameena cried.

'Nothing! I didn't do anything!'

Another sound, like the smash of a wrecking ball, vibrated the floor beneath us. The squeals of the screechers rose in volume, but they faded again just as quickly. The hammering on the door stopped, and as we listened we heard the screechers fleeing the house. Their screams grew quieter still as they clattered off into the distance.

'They've gone,' Billy whispered, when the house had gone quiet once more. We leaned there in the V-shape between the floor and the wall, listening to the sound of silence.

'Have they?' Rosie asked, her eyes wide with hope. She looked to me. 'Have they gone?'

'I... uh... I don't know,' I admitted. 'It sounds like they have.'

With a *crack*, the door to the box room exploded outward. The screechers downstairs might have left, but the policewoman hadn't gone with them. She threw back her head and screamed. Her black eyes locked on us and her teeth chewed hungrily as she clattered on all fours down the slope towards us.

The spike burst through the floor directly in front of her, stabbing up from below. She twisted, mid-leap, but the javelin-like bone speared her through the stomach. Blood frothed around her mouth as she was pulled through the floorboards and down into the darkened room below.

'Stay there,' I barked at Billy and Rosie, as I clambered up to the hole in the floor. Ameena got to it just as I did. We looked through it in time to see the policewoman's mutated body tear in two.

Eyes the size of our heads swivelled to look at us from behind their protective bone-cages. The Beast's mouth opened wide and its thunderous roar knocked us back away from the hole.

'Well, the kids are gone,' Ameena said hoarsely. 'But looks like daddy's home.'

The floorboards splintered again as another spike broke through from beneath. It stabbed up between Billy's legs, stopping just centimetres short of his crotch. Billy gave a squeal and jumped sideways, clutching his groin protectively.

'Ooh, that could've been nasty,' Ameena said.

CRACK! The spike withdrew, then jabbed up through the floorboards again. It split the wood at Rosie's feet. She slid down the sloping floor, only stopping when her back slammed against the equally sloping wall.

'We have *got* to get out of here,' Billy hissed.

There was another door just a few metres up the incline. I knew from our exploration earlier that it led to another bedroom. With the house leaning the way it was, it should be possible to jump through the bedroom window and land safely in the snow. After that, all we had to do was outrun the Beast, dodge the screechers, track down Nan, then find a way to get out of the village.

Yeah. That was all.

I locked my eyes on the door. One step at a time. Escape first. I could worry about the other stuff later.

The floor wobbled unsteadily as I inched my way towards the bedroom. 'Stay close to me,' I urged. 'We'll get out this wa-*aaaaay!*'

My words became a scream of terror as the wall of the house gave way. The floor dropped out from under us and we fell through into the living room. Clouds of dust and plaster swirled up into the air, filling the room with a choking stour.

'Ameena?' I coughed. The dust was thick. It whitened my hair and forced closed my eyes. I clambered to my feet, relieved – and surprised – to discover I was unhurt. 'Billy? Rosie? Where are you?'

WREEEEEEEEEK!

The cry of the Beast was right in front of me, half lion-like roar, half pig-squeal. A gust of its hot breath hit me in the face. It blew some of the dust from my eyes, allowing me to open them.

Big mistake.

The Beast's face was centimetres from my own. Up close, it looked even more monstrous. Its skull, from the top of its head to the tip of its chin, was deformed and misshapen, with lumps and bumps here, there and everywhere.

Slivers of bone poked out from the face and jutted up from the neck. A stubby spike stuck out from the centre of its forehead, like the horn of the world's ugliest unicorn.

It was the same creature we'd seen earlier, only it had grown. The shape we'd seen in the fog had been rhino-sized. This was bigger. *Much* bigger. Its back was bent and its head lowered as it glared down at me. I could see more of the serrated, bony spikes running the length of its spine. More bones jutted from its elbows and knees, sharp and yellowing and stained with blood.

I felt another blast of the Beast's foul breath, and watched as a mouthful of green mucus dribbled down its chin. No wonder the screechers had turned and fled.

Slowly, I back-paced away from the monster. It padded forward on all four feet, closing the gap, but not yet moving to attack. The back feet, I noticed, had three toes, just like the footprint we'd seen in Mrs Angelo's house. The two at the front were more like hands. They were bunched into fists. The creature walked on them like a gorilla would, leaning forward, balancing on the knuckles.

I stopped retreating and the Beast stopped advancing.

We stood there, half a metre apart, me looking up and it looking down. Its slow breathing was like the wind on a stormy night. It rattled from the back of its throat. In, *two, three, four*, out, *two, three, four*.

The black, shark-like eyes were trained on my face. I leaned slowly to the right and the creature's head swivelled to follow me. I leaned back to the centre, then out to the left, tracked the entire time by the monster's glare.

There was a *clatter* from behind it and the Beast's eyes narrowed to slits. It gave a low growl and, even from that distance, I could feel its whole body tense.

Ameena shoved aside a pile of broken floorboards and stood up. She froze when she saw me, and even through the dust that was caked to her face, I could see the last of the colour drain from her cheeks.

'It's OK,' I said, keeping my voice low and my gaze fixed on the Beast's eyes. 'It's just... looking at me.'

Ameena gave a slow nod. There was a commotion beside her and Billy's arm emerged from the debris. The

Beast's head twitched and its dense muscles became like coiled springs as Ameena pulled Billy free.

'Relax,' I said softly. I half-expected the monster to lunge then, but instead some of the tension seemed to leave its body. Its jaws, which had been hanging open, very slowly closed over.

The Beast wasn't attacking me. For whatever reason, it wasn't attacking me! I decided to push my luck. Very carefully, I raised my left hand, palm-forwards, into the air. I held it up there, just fifteen centimetres or so from the monster's head. The Beast's black eyes moved from my face to my hand. It gave a low, suspicious growl. Then, with a sudden bob of its head, it nudged my palm with its nose. I kept my hand up, ignoring the sticky strands of mucus now hanging from my fingers.

Slowly, almost cautiously, it pressed its snout against the hand again. This time it didn't move away. Its dark eyes closed over and a low sound formed somewhere at the back of its throat.

Kaaaaaa.

The Beast's nose pressed harder against my hand. I almost felt my nerve go, but I managed to keep my arm up. I even managed to keep it from trembling too badly.

Kaaaaaahhhhh.

'What's it doing?' Billy asked, his voice hushed.

'I don't know,' I said, not shifting my gaze from the Beast's broad face.

The snout nuzzled even more firmly against the palm of my hand. The Beast's mouth opened and I felt the warmth of its breath as another sound emerged.

Kaaaaaaahhhhhhhlll.

I heard Ameena draw in a sharp breath. 'Was that...? Did that just...?' I knew then that she'd heard the same thing as I had, and that she was having just as much trouble believing it. 'Tell me it didn't just say your name.'

A sudden scream shattered the spell. The Beast's eyes snapped open and my hand jerked back. It let out a ferocious snarl and its deformed face twisted with rage.

'Rosie, *stop*,' I warned, tearing my gaze from the monster and looking over to where the blonde-haired girl had climbed free of the debris. She didn't hear me, just screamed even more loudly as the creature spun on the spot to face her.

'Run!' I bellowed. 'All of you, run!'

'We'll never outrun *that*!' Billy wailed. Rosie stopped screaming when Ameena's hand clamped over her mouth.

'Yes you will,' I said. 'My turn to distract it.'

Ameena shook her head. 'Kyle, no! You can't!'

The Beast lunged forwards. I saw its teeth *clack* together and its trailing mucus spray out in a wide circle.

'I can,' I assured her. 'Go. I'll be fine.'

She hesitated, one hand still held over Rosie's mouth. 'Promise?'

I nodded. 'Promise.'

And before she could try to talk me out of it, I threw myself at the Beast, and scrambled up on to its broad, armoured back.

Chapter Eighteen

ALONE TOGETHER

The spikes that covered the monster's back looked like perfect handholds. They weren't. They were sharp and rough all the way down their length, and it was all I could do to avoid accidentally gutting myself like a fish.

'Wait. Stop!' I cried, as the Beast set off after Ameena and the others. They were running back towards the centre of the village, heads down, legs pumping through the snow. They were still too close, though. I had to buy them more time.

My hands held tightly to the Beast's bulging ears. The soles of my feet pressed flat against its back, as I tried to stay away from those deadly spikes. A jolt shot through my legs as it bounded forward. My grip slipped and I cried out in pain as one of the blade-like bones cut into my thigh.

I rolled sideways, fell face-first, and wound up eating snow. Raising my head, I saw the Beast galloping on, leaving me behind, gaining ground on the others.

Gritting my teeth against the pain the movement brought, I stood up. The Beast was already almost too far away. I'd only get one chance at this. I had to make it count.

Whispering a silent prayer to anyone who cared to listen, I drew back my arm and let fly with a snowball.

BAD-OOOSH!

The hard-packed snow disintegrated against the back of the Beast's skull. It turned, startled, and bit back over its shoulder. Finding no one there, it kept spinning, searching for whoever had attacked it.

I ducked behind a car and watched the Beast through the windscreen. My plan had been to draw the monster back towards me, but things had worked out even better than I'd hoped. It was still just turning in sharp circles, like a dog chasing its tail, trying to figure out what the hell had just happened.

Every second it spent spinning was another second Ameena and the others had to get away. They were three dots at the bottom of the hill now. The route they were running would lead them past the church. If I knew Ameena, they'd hunker down and wait for me there. All I had to do was find a way past the Beast.

Luckily, the Beast made it easy. By the time it eventually stopped turning, it seemed to have forgotten why it had started in the first place. It snorted noisily a few times, like a racehorse after a sprint finish, pawed at the ground, then sloped off into the shadows between two buildings.

I kept watching, waiting for it to reappear. I hung back there behind the car for five or six minutes, the snow numbing the pain from the wound on my leg. Thankfully, the cut wasn't deep – little more than a shallow scratch, really – and it didn't bother me too much when I hurried down the hill towards the church.

* * *

The church doors were closed when I arrived. I *creaked* them open and tiptoed my way inside. The little entrance foyer was empty. I crossed it and nudged open the swing doors.

The moment the door opened, I heard the screechers. The sound was coming from the little hall where I'd made my escape earlier. They were still in there, battering against the closed door, trying to chase me down.

Quietly, I let the door close over, and returned to the street outside. I pulled the outer doors closed again, trapping the screechers inside. Ameena and the others weren't there. So, where were they?

PAF!

A snowball exploded against the wall beside me. I ducked low, scanning the area for any sign of who'd thrown it.

PAF!

Another one hit the wall directly above where I was standing, and I felt droplets of cold spray down on me from above. I looked in the direction the snowball had come from, and saw Billy standing in the darkened doorway of a house across the street. He gestured for me to come over.

Pausing only to check the coast was clear, I dashed across the road. I was barely a third of the way across when a shriek of rage rebounded off the walls on either side of the street.

Billy pointed behind me. His mouth flapped open and closed and I heard him stammer something I couldn't make out. An upstairs window of the house was dragged open and Ameena's head emerged.

'Kyle, *run!*' she hollered. She needn't have bothered. My legs were already pumping at full pace as I desperately tried to reach the house before the screecher reached me.

Billy retreated back inside the hallway, and for a moment I was sure he was about to slam the door shut. But he emerged again a moment later, clutching a large kitchen knife in his hand.

The sight of Billy with a knife sent chills the length of my spine. Last time I'd seen him with a blade, he'd stuck it in me. This time, though, he let out a roar and moved to charge past me as I raced along the front path.

The screecher howled just a few metres behind us. Billy spun as I caught him by the arm and I thought, from the look on his face, that he really was about to kill me.

'Let go!' he hissed. 'Let me do this.'

'N-no,' I stammered, dragging him towards the door. 'It'll tear you apart, get inside.'

He only half resisted, and I dragged him into the house with the screecher hot on our heels. 'Close the door!' he yelped, all thoughts of bravery apparently having slipped away.

I did as he said and shut the door. At least, I tried to. But the screecher was too close, too strong, moving too fast. The door flew open, knocking me backwards, just as a hulking shape burst into the room.

His eyes were black, like the others. A chunk of flesh had been bitten from his neck. Blood pumped from the wound, staining his clothes a dark, dirty red. His bottom jaw jutted outwards, so his lower teeth were in front of his upper ones. Otherwise, though, he looked exactly the same as before.

'Huggs?' Ameena gasped. She had raced down the stairs and now stood at the bottom, staring in disbelief at the figure before us.

His head whipped round at the sound. His black eyes became angry, narrow slits and an animal roar rolled from within his throat.

'I told you, *don't* wind him up!' Billy whimpered.

Too late. Guggs made a dive for Ameena, swiping at her with fingers that looked more like claws. She tried to dodge, but the stairway was a tight space with no room to manoeuvre. He caught her by the hair and by the throat and she landed hard on the steps behind her.

Ameena's arms braced against Guggs' head. Her muscles strained and her back arched as she fought to force him off her. His distended jaw snapped open and closed, trying to bite through the closest arm.

I grabbed for Guggs' shoulders, trying to pull him back.

An elbow fired backwards. It caught me across the cheek and I felt pain explode through my skull.

The world spun as I moved again to pull him off her. This time, I dug a hand into the gaping wound on his neck. He let out a shriek and turned on me, his dark eyes blazing hatred.

Ameena lay on the stairs, coughing and spluttering as she fought to get her breath back. I saw her hold a hand above her head, heard her croak, 'Rosie, gimme that,' but then Guggs was at me and I could see and hear nothing but him.

Billy let out a cry that was bordering on madness. He took a step forward and swung back with his arm. *'That's for making me leave Lily!'* he screamed, as he plunged the kitchen knife into Guggs' thigh.

The monster that had been Billy's cousin staggered and let out another blood-curdling screech. He didn't fall, though, but turned to Billy instead. The blade through his leg didn't slow him as he caught hold of Billy and slammed him backwards on to the floor.

I moved to drag him off, but Ameena shoved past me. 'I warned you, Huggs,' she growled, and it was then that I saw the golf club in her hand. Guggs turned, snarled, opened his gaping mouth wide. Ameena swung back the club. 'Touch me again and I'll kill you.'

CLUNK!

The club connected hard with Guggs' head, sending him sprawling sideways off Billy. He thudded on to the carpet and lay there, not moving.

'Howzat?' Ameena said.

'Wrong game,' I told her, staring down at the motionless body. '*Howzat*'s what they say in cricket.'

She wiped a bead of sweat from her brow. 'Oh,' she muttered. 'Well... home run?'

I nodded. 'Close enough.'

Billy was standing up again, staying behind me, well away from his fallen cousin. He looked over to Ameena and gave her a nod. 'Th-thanks,' he said.

Ameena shrugged. She lowered the club and leaned

on it, like a golf champion posing for a victory photograph. 'Ah, forget it,' she said. 'It was noth—'

Guggs' head raised. His jaw opened then clamped shut. The bottom half of the golf club flopped to the floor, leaving Ameena holding just the rubber grip.

In one fluid movement, Billy's cousin sprang back to his feet. He screamed and writhed as spear-like bones tore through the skin of his forearms. The pain kept him from attacking us, but I knew it wouldn't last.

'Move, get out!' I yelped, pushing Ameena towards the door.

'Rosie's upstairs,' Billy said.

I called her name. 'Rosie! *Rosie!*' She didn't reply. 'I'll get her,' I said, taking the stairs two-at-a-time. 'Get out. Get somewhere safe. I'll find you. Somehow.'

'The radio!' Billy cried. I reached for my hip. The walkie-talkie was still clipped to my belt. With a twist of the knob, I switched it on.

'Good idea. *Go!*'

Billy was already out the door. Ameena bounced on the spot, trying to decide what to do. But the bones had stopped growing from Guggs' arms and his squeals were gradually dying away. There was no time for argument.

As I reached the top of the stairs, I saw Ameena bolt for the door, leaving Billy's cousin twisting and writhing in the hall.

'Rosie?' I said, my voice low and urgent. 'Rosie, where are you?'

The upstairs landing of the house had three doors, all closed. I pushed the first one open. Empty. The second one resisted as I tried to force my way inside.

'Rosie, it's me!' I hissed. From beyond the door, there was only silence. I tried shoving it open again, and heard a strangled sob from the other side. Down in the hall, Guggs' screams finally fell silent.

'Rosie, please,' I urged. 'Open up. Let me in. I can't protect you if you don't let me inside.'

Again, there was no reply. But then, from the other side

of the door, I heard Rosie take a step back. I pushed down the handle and the door swung open. Stumbling inside, I quickly closed it behind me again, just as a heavy pair of feet began racing up the stairs.

'The bed,' I said, 'help me move the bed.'

Rosie's eyes were ringed with red. She didn't speak, just nodded. Together, we shoved the room's double bed in front of the door, jamming it shut. Beyond the door, Guggs arrived on the empty landing and let out a howl of confusion and rage.

I climbed on to the bed, pressed my ear to the door, and listened to him skulking around. The upstairs hallway had laminate flooring. His footsteps clomped across it, irregular and uneven.

Rosie backed further into the room, biting on her sleeve to stop herself screaming. I held my breath, listened to the *thunk, thunk, thunk* of his steps, until they stopped right outside the door.

I backed away and jumped down from the bed, expecting one of those spikes to split the wood at any moment. I was still watching the door when I felt Rosie's breath by my ear.

'Alone at last,' she whispered.

'Well, we're not *that* alone,' I replied. Something hammered loudly against the door, and I took another step back. 'God, he's keen, isn't he?'

I jumped with fright when Rosie's arms slipped beneath mine. They wrapped across my chest until she was hugging me from behind.

'I never did thank you properly for getting me out,' she said.

My cheeks went pink. I tried to take a deep breath, but her arms were coiled too tightly around me. 'It was nothing,' I told her. 'Forget it.'

THUD. Guggs struck the door again, but it was Rosie who was making my heart beat faster and faster.

'So modest,' she purred. 'A true hero.'

'Um... maybe we should talk about this another time?' I suggested.

Rosie giggled softly in my ear. 'It's OK. He'll get fed

up and go after the others in a minute. I don't think he likes your ex-girlfriend much.'

'She's not my... wait. *Ex*-girlfriend?'

'Well, of course, pumpkin,' Rosie said, hugging me tighter. '*I'm* your girlfriend now.' Her voice took on an excited edge. 'I wonder what he'll do to her when he catches her? Whatever it is, I hope it's painful, the *witch*.'

'What?' I muttered. I tried to pull away again, but her arms were like steel bands around my chest. 'What are you—?'

'She doesn't appreciate you. Not like I do. She made fun of you. The little witch *laughed* at you!'

'Rosie,' I grimaced. 'Stop. You're... you're hurting me.'

BANG! The door shook in its frame. *BANG!* Guggs, it seemed, wasn't going anywhere.

Rosie's grip relaxed and I heard her give a sigh of annoyance. 'Why won't people just leave us in peace?' she demanded. 'First it's *your* friends, then it's *mine*.'

She stomped over to the door. I watched in horror as she pushed the bed aside and reached for the handle.

'No, don't! What are you—?'

I was too late to stop her. She yanked open the door just as Guggs launched himself towards it. He gave a screech of triumph as he flew into the room and landed right beside Rosie.

A moment later, the sound died in his throat when Rosie jammed her fingertips against the centre of his chest. Guggs' eyes went wide. His neck snapped down in time to see Rosie push her fingertips straight through his chest bone.

Billy's cousin made a low, gargling sound as Rosie withdrew her hand. His legs went limp and he fell awkwardly on to the floor. In Rosie's hand, Guggs' heart pumped twice, then stopped forever.

'Now, pumpkin,' beamed Rosie, letting the organ drop to the floor with a *schlup*. 'Where were we?'

Chapter Nineteen

BATTLE OF THE BEASTS

Billy's voice squawked from my hip as Rosie slowly closed the bedroom door. 'Kyle? You there? We're back at the police station, up on the roof, over.'

'Don't answer it,' Rosie said. She ran her fingers through her long, blonde hair as she stepped over Guggs' broken body, leaving a bloody streak right across her scalp. 'Let it just be you and me for a while.'

'What... what *are* you?'

She half-smiled, half-frowned. 'What a strange thing to ask,' she said. 'I'm your *girlfriend*, you silly sausage.'

'Oi! You there or what?' Ameena's voice hissed over the radio. 'Answer us, will you?'

'You're supposed to say "over",' Billy's voice explained in the background.

'Shut up, Billy.'

Rosie's face had grown darker with every word.

'Why won't they be quiet?' she spat. 'Why won't they leave us in peace?'

'They're worried about... us,' I explained.

I recoiled as Rosie reached towards me, but all she did was flip the walkie-talkie's off switch, silencing the voices on the other end.

She smiled. 'So let them worry.'

'You're one of *them*, aren't you? An imaginary friend. From the Darkest Corners.'

'What does it matter where I'm from? All that matters is that we're together at last.'

'My dad sent you, didn't he?'

Rosie nodded slowly. 'But he didn't tell me how cute you were.'

She tried to put a hand on my face, but I pulled sharply

away. 'So, what? He brought you and the Beast here together? To kill everyone?'

'No, silly,' she giggled. 'He brought me and I made the Beast.'

'You... made it?' I frowned. 'But how?'

Rosie chomped her teeth together, answering my question.

'And what about the others? The screechers? You made them too?'

'A few,' she nodded. 'Then they made others, and those others made others still. It's like a virus, see? Passing from one to the other.'

Her delicate features pulled into a frown. 'And if your ex really *was* bitten, then she should've changed already. What's up with *that*?' A thought occurred to her. 'Bet she was just looking for sympathy from you. Bet she faked the whole thing so you'd give her a hug.'

Rosie curled her fingers in until her nails left half-moon-shaped marks on her palms. 'Ooh, she makes me so mad,'

Rosie spat. 'Don't worry, pumpkin. First chance I get, I'm going to tear that witch's heart out.'

'No, you won't,' I said.

Rosie glared at me. 'What?'

'You're not going to touch her. I won't let you.'

She gave a sharp shake of her head. 'Tell me... Tell me you don't still *care* about her.'

'Yes,' I said. 'I do.'

'But, but, but you're *my* boyfriend, not hers!'

'No,' I said. 'I'm not.'

'But I appreciate you. She doesn't. She makes fun of you!'

I shrugged. 'At least she's real.'

'*I'm* real, pumpkin,' Rosie said.

'No,' I said. 'You aren't. And that story about your parents. That wasn't real either, was it? You made it all up.'

She didn't answer me.

'Thought so,' I said. My heart crashed against the inside of my chest as I moved to go past her. 'Now, if you don't mind, I'm going to go and find my friends.'

'Mind?' she cried, and her voice became a shriek. '*Of course I mind!* Don't you *dare* walk out on me!'

'I'm going, Rosie,' I told her. My hand closed around the handle of the door. 'Deal with it.'

'You're not going *anywhere*!' she said, and her shriek became a screech. She covered the gap between us in a fraction of a second. Her hand clamped down on top of mine, squashing it against the door handle. The colour drained from her eyes and they became a rich, oily black.

Her hand was changing shape when it pressed against my chest. The fingers were widening, the knuckles becoming sharp, ragged bone. She gave a grunt and shoved me. The room passed in a blur as I was propelled away from the door. My back struck the wall and I dropped to my knees, winded.

Get up, screamed my brain, but my legs struggled to obey. At the other end of the bedroom, Rosie was also down on the floor. She was hidden by the bed, but the cracking of bone and the tearing of flesh and the sound of her frenzied screams told me a very different Rosie was about to get back up.

A chill draught rolled in through the window. Shakily, I placed my hands on the sill and pulled myself to my feet. A small porch with a slanted slate roof sat just outside.

As Rosie continued to writhe on the floor, I clambered through the open window and let myself fall on to the porch roof. The slates were slippery and I lost my footing right away. My bum thumped against the roof, and then I was falling. The snow proved to be an effective cushion again, and I escaped unhurt from the drop.

My legs were still unsteady as I began to run in the direction of the police station. My hands fumbled for the walkie-talkie as I ran. 'Ameena. Billy. You there?'

Nothing. Then a crackle. Then, 'Finally,' Ameena said. 'Where are you?'

'Heading your way!'

Static hissed at me for a moment, before Ameena's voice broke in again. 'You can't come here. Turn back. You hear me?'

I heard Billy's scream in stereo – over the radio and from just around the corner. Ameena swore, then there was a clatter, and then there was nothing but the soft crackle of static.

'Ameena?' I said, jabbing the speak button. *'Ameena? Answer me.'*

KA-RAAASH!

The bedroom window and part of the wall behind me erupted. A snarling, screeching monstrosity landed on all fours in the garden, making the ground tremble beneath my feet.

I hurled myself on, tripping and tumbling through the snowdrifts. I had to get to the police station. Had to get away from the monster that had been Rosie. Had to make sure Ameena was...

Was...

The police station was half-buried beneath an onslaught of screechers. They were there in their hundreds, battering against the walls, throwing themselves through what remained of the glass doors.

There were even some on the roof. I could see Billy and Ameena swinging at them, knocking them back, but there were more climbing up on all sides, and others still behind them.

Some of the screechers were bent double, howling and screaming, the bones erupting through their flesh as they changed – evolved – into Beasts.

I stopped. There was no point running now. There was nowhere left to run to. Instead I turned around, and got my first proper look at the thing that Rosie had become.

It looked like the Beast, only a new and improved model. Its head and body were bigger, its limbs longer, the muscles more defined. An exoskeleton of ragged grey bone almost covered it completely. Other bones jutted from its joints like machete blades, each one more lethal-looking than the last.

The mouth was made up of four sections. They all opened outwards as the creature launched itself at me, revealing four complete rows of saw-like teeth. A shock of electricity zapped through me. It took every ounce of my willpower to push it away. My dad needed me to use my powers so he could unleash the Darkest Corners on the world. This, all this, was just a taster of what would happen if I did. So I wouldn't. I wouldn't help him. I wouldn't give in.

Even if it meant dying.

I held up my hands, ducked down, screwed shut my eyes. The monster roared as it descended on me, closing in for the kill. In the darkness behind my eyelids, I heard another sound – another roar, just as wild and as savage as the first.

Opening my eyes, I saw not one but two monsters, joined together, each one tearing and clawing at the other.

They crunched on to the snow in front of me, then bounced over my head. They were still spitting and swiping at one another as they rolled and spun down the hill towards the police station.

The sound of the Beasts scattered the screechers. They fell and leapt and clambered over one another in their hurry to escape the approaching monsters. Not that the monsters had noticed them. They were too busy fighting, too locked in battle to notice anything else going on around them.

Up on the rooftop, Ameena kicked the last of the screechers off, then snatched up her walkie-talkie. 'What the hell's going on?' her voice hissed at me. 'Why's there two of them?'

'One of them's Rosie,' I explained. 'The bigger one.'

'I *knew* there was something dodgy about that girl! No one cries that much.' Ameena almost sounded pleased. 'Not so pretty now, is she?'

'The mucus is a bit off-putting, yeah,' I said.

'How come they're fighting?'

I hesitated, my finger held over the talk button. Eventually, I pressed it. 'The Beast... saved me.'

A static buzz, then: 'Why?'

I considered just coming out with it, but decided I should build up to it gently first. 'I thought the Beast was the one biting people and turning them into screechers, but it isn't. It's Rosie. She's the monster. *She* bit someone and turned them into that thing. The Beast, it was just Rosie's first victim.'

I hesitated again. I didn't want to believe what I was about to say, but what choice did I have? It was the only answer that made sense. 'Or rather, *she* was the first victim.'

The monsters rolled apart and turned to face one another. The Beast – the first one – stood with its back to me, blocking me from "Rosie's" view. It was crouching low, its limbs tensed, ready to leap into battle.

'I thought whatever had attacked the policewoman had taken Nan prisoner, but... these things don't take prisoners. You either outrun them or you die, and Joseph told me Nan wasn't dead.'

The walkie-talkie gave a crackle. 'You're not saying what I think you're saying?'

I looked across to the monster that had just saved my life. 'I... I think I am,' I said, nodding slowly. 'The Beast didn't take my nan. The Beast *is* my nan.'

Chapter Twenty

THE FINAL STRAW

The Rosie-monster let out a bellowing cry, drowning out most of Ameena's response.

'...what you saying? Your nan's brain's in that thing?' was all I caught.

I watched the Beast snap and snarl, trying to scare its opponent into running away. 'I don't think so,' I replied. 'The screechers, they've all lost their minds, and I think so has Nan. Mostly. But there must be a part of it in there that recognises me, or something. She's a monster, but a monster who doesn't want to see me get hurt.'

'That's convenient.' I could suddenly hear Ameena's voice in both ears. I turned to find her hurrying up behind me, with Billy at her heels.

The creatures screeched and howled as they resumed their fight. Rosie was bigger and more powerful, but the Beast was fast. It slashed out with a bony spike just as Rosie charged towards it. The blade pierced Rosie's shoulder and was driven deep in by the monster's weight.

'Way to go, Kyle's nan,' Ameena whistled, but she had spoken too soon.

There was a loud *krik* of breaking bone and the Beast let out an agonised howl. Rosie pressed forward, appearing not to notice the spike sticking out of her shoulder. Her fist slammed like a sledgehammer against the Beast's chin, flipping it on to its back. It shrieked again as its weight snapped the spikes that jutted out from its spine.

Rosie was on it in a heartbeat, thundering more blows against its head, slashing it with her bony blades. Thick, oily blood began to stain the snow around them, and Rosie threw back her head and howled in triumph.

'She's killing her,' I realised. 'She's going to kill her!'

I moved to run forwards, to help, but Billy caught me

and held me back. 'You can't!' he told me. 'You can't get in the middle of that, you'll be killed.'

'Get off, Billy,' I growled. 'I'm not just leaving her.'

'Of course not,' Billy said. He gave me a curt nod and let go of my arm. 'But just... let's be careful. I've got your back.'

He extended a hand to me. I shook it without hesitation. 'Thanks, Billy,' I said.

'Can we save the bromance, please?' Ameena said. 'Kyle's nan. Fighting a monster. Remember?' She shook her head. 'God, my life just gets weirder and weirder.'

'Um... OK, here's the plan,' I said. 'Ameena, stick next to me.'

'What about me?' Billy asked.

'Snowballs,' I said.

Billy raised his eyebrows. 'Snowballs?'

'Hit the big one with it. Pelt it as hard as you can.'

'Why?'

'To get its attention. To annoy it.' I patted him on the shoulder. 'I know you can do annoying, Billy.'

'Maybe I should do the snowballs?' Ameena suggested. 'I'm a better aim. Billy and I should swap.'

'No!' I said quickly. 'Definitely not! Billy, snowballs, Ameena with me.'

Billy hesitated. 'But... but what if it comes after me?'

'That's the entire point,' I told him, then darted off before he could complain.

Rosie was still pounding on the Beast. She raised both arms above her head then brought them down hard. The Beast squealed as Rosie's exoskeleton smashed hard against its face.

'Now, Billy!' I hissed. I'd pulled Ameena off to one side, out of Rosie's direct line of sight. Billy wasn't so lucky. He was standing directly in front of her. All she had to do was raise her head and she'd be looking straight at him.

Billy, to his credit, did as he was told. Crouching, he hurriedly pressed together half a dozen snowballs and cradled them in the crook of his left arm. With his right he picked up the first one, took aim, and threw.

The snowball landed silently in the snow beside the writhing bodies of the battling Beasts.

PAF! The second one found a target, but it was the wrong one. Pinned below Rosie, the Beast gave a growl as the snowball splattered across its head.

'He's useless,' Ameena muttered. 'I'm swapping places.'

'No, you can't,' I told her, holding her back. 'I need you here with me.'

'Why? What for?'

I felt my lips go dry. 'Um... you'll find out.'

The third snowball exploded against the Rosie-monster's chest. Billy recoiled in horror, getting ready to run. But she kept pummelling on the Beast, clawing at it, biting at it, and Billy took aim once again.

PAF! The snowball struck her right in the centre of her face. Her head snapped up and her black eyes became slits as she locked on to Billy.

'Um... hi,' he whimpered, and then he dropped the remaining snowballs, turned on his heels, and ran.

With a kick of her back legs, Rosie set off in pursuit.

Billy screamed as he ran. He dodged between cars, only for them to be flattened beneath Rosie's immense weight.

'She's going to kill him,' Ameena winced. 'She's too fast.'

I hurried over to the Beast. It – *she* – lay on her back in the blood-slicked snow, barely moving. Barely alive.

'Hold on, Nan,' I said softly. I rummaged in the snow beside her until I'd found what I was looking for. 'You're going to be OK.'

I ran back over to Ameena, struggling with the weight of the object in my hands. 'What are you doing with that?' she asked.

'No time to explain,' I said. I felt my cheeks prickle red. 'And, um, whatever happens next, don't hit me, OK?'

Her eyes narrowed. 'No promises.'

'Right,' I nodded. My hands were shaking and my head felt light at the thought of what I was about to do. 'Here goes.' I put a hand to the side of my mouth, took a deep breath, and shouted as loudly as I could. 'Hey, Rosie!'

Across the street, Rosie had just begun tearing through

a fence Billy was using to hide behind. At the sound of my voice, she stopped. 'Over here!' I cried, waving one hand above my head. With the other, I wedged the thing I was holding into the snow between our feet.

Rosie's face drew back into a snarl. She began to advance slowly. That was no use. I needed her running, charging at me, full speed. I'd hoped I might not need to put the second part of my plan into action, but it looked like Rosie was leaving me with no choice.

'I just wanted to let you know...' I began. With my free hand I grabbed Ameena by the front of her coat, pulled her in close to me, and kissed her. Her lips were cold and chapped and her eyes were wide with surprise. As first kisses went, it probably wasn't an all-time classic, but considering the circumstances, I could be pretty sure I'd remember it for the rest of my life.

I leaned back, flashed Ameena an apologetic smile, then turned to the Rosie-monster, '...you're dumped.'

That did it. She set off like a racehorse from the stalls, splitting the night with her terrible screech. The ground shook beneath us. The snow bounced into the air, as her colossal feet pounded against the pavement.

With a final, blood-curdling scream she launched herself towards us, arms splayed wide. Shoving hard, I sent Ameena stumbling backwards. At the same time, I threw myself clear, leaving only the long broken spike of the Beast's bone sticking up from the ground.

Rosie's black eyes widened as the spear-like point pierced the centre of her chest. There was a *crack*, then a scream, then the sound of something wet being torn in two. The bone burst through Rosie's back and she hit the ground, face-first.

For a moment, she flailed around, coughing and gargling as her life ebbed out on to the snow. And then, like that, she stopped.

'I don't believe it,' Ameena said, her voice a hushed whisper.

'We did it,' I nodded.

'What? Oh yeah, that,' she nodded. 'But I meant... *You kissed me!*'

I turned to look at her, trying to read her face. 'Yes. I did. Sorry.'

She nodded. 'So you should be,' she said. She punched me on the arm, but I couldn't help but notice she didn't hit me nearly as hard as she usually did.

'We did it,' I said again. 'And I didn't even have to use my powers.'

'Still the little problem of the infected villagers,' Ameena reminded me.

I sighed. 'Don't spoil it.'

Billy ran up to join us. He was breathing heavily and his face was as white as the snow. 'Did I do good?' he asked hopefully.

'You were great, Billy,' I said, but my attention was now on the creature that had once been my nan. Her breathing was shallow, her body awash with blood from her many gaping wounds.

Before I could approach her, though, I heard a slow hand-clapping from somewhere behind us. I turned and an all-too-familiar face smirked back at me.

'Bravo,' my dad said. He was on his own, strolling casually through the snow towards us. 'You did it, son. You actually did it.'

'Son?' Ameena muttered. 'You mean, that's...?'

I nodded. 'What do you want?'

'Oh, just to congratulate you, that's all,' he shrugged. 'You said you wouldn't use your abilities and you didn't. You proved me wrong.'

'I know,' I said. 'I'm not going to help you. Face it. You've lost.'

He nodded in the direction of the Beast. A grim smile played at the corners of his mouth. 'Looks like I'm not the only one,' he said. His expression became one of mock concern. 'Did I follow things right? Is that *really* your grandmother trapped in there? I can't imagine how upsetting that must be for you. Watching her die. As a monster. I can't imagine.' He cracked a smile. 'Oh, who am I kidding? Of course I can imagine. I'm the one who arranged for her to be at your house, called the police, the whole thing. All so our little Rosie could turn her into *that*.'

He blew on his fingernails and wiped them against his checked shirt. 'Of course, you could always change her back.'

I felt my stomach tighten. 'What?'

'With your special gift,' he continued, smiling innocently. 'You could change her back. Fix her. You could fix everyone. Your nan. His sister. Everyone.'

I felt Billy go tense. 'Lily? You could... you could help Lily?'

I shook my head. 'I... I...'

My dad strolled over to where the Beast lay. She flinched, but only a little, when he rested his hand against her bruised and bloodied head. 'Oh, what to do?' he smirked. 'What to do?'

'Back off, scumbag,' Ameena growled. 'Go and crawl back under whatever rock you came from.'

He fixed her with a long, lingering look. 'You must be

Ameena,' he said, at last. 'I've heard so much about you. In fact, I heard you got yourself bitten today.' He scratched his head. 'I wonder why you didn't change,' he said. 'Isn't that odd?'

He took a pace towards her. 'Then again, that's not the only odd thing about you, is it, Ameena? It's odd, for example, the way you just turned up out of the blue like that to save my son here from Mr Mumbles.' He looked at me. 'That's odd, isn't it?'

I shook my head. 'No, it's—'

'It's odd how you became so loyal so quickly. How you would give your life for a boy you barely know.'

'What?' she muttered. 'What are you...?'

'It's also odd that when he is scared, you are brave. When he is down, you raise him up. When he is lost, you're there to find him. It's almost like...' A shimmer of dark delight shone behind his eyes. '...you were *made* for him.'

He let the sentence hang there in the cold and in the dark.

'And you,' he said to me. 'You trust her so much, and yet you know nothing about her. What's her last name, for example?'

I would've loved to tell him, to wipe the smug grin off his face, but I realised that I had no idea what Ameena's last name was.

'Don't know?' he asked. He turned to Ameena. 'Go on then, you tell him. Tell us all. What's your last name?'

Ameena opened her mouth. A look of panic flashed across her face, but then it was gone, replaced by her usual sneer. 'None of your business.'

'When were you born, Ameena? What's your date of birth?'

She didn't say anything, but there was that worried look again.

'No? Let's try something less challenging, then. Tell me, what were you doing before you hit Mr Mumbles with that baseball bat? Where were you going? Where had you been?'

Ameena stumbled around for an answer. 'I was... I was...'

My dad turned and loomed over me. 'In the garage, when you needed a light, you created a light. When you needed a weapon, you made one from nothing. A shield. A mattress. Even a dog. When you needed all these things most, your mind reached out and it made them. It made them.'

He jabbed a finger towards Ameena. 'Just like it made *her*.'

I shook my head. I turned to Ameena, but she didn't meet my gaze.

'N-no,' I stammered. 'She's real. She's real.'

Ameena's mouth flapped open and closed. 'I don't remember,' she whispered. 'My name. Or... or how old I am. I... I don't remember anything.'

'No!' I insisted. 'You're real. *She's real!* She's not... She's not an imaginary friend.'

'You're damn right she's not!' my dad said, his voice raised. '*I* was an imaginary friend.' He pointed to the fallen body that had once been Rosie. '*She* was an imaginary friend.'

Ameena raised her head and looked my dad in the eye. 'So... So what *am* I?'

'You're a *thing*,' he told her, taking great delight in the way her face fell. 'You're an *object*, like the axe, or the lightbulb. You're not a person, not even an imaginary one. You're a *tool* designed to do a job. That's all.'

'You're the only tool around here, mate,' Billy said, but my dad didn't acknowledge he'd even spoken.

Somewhere, not too far away, I heard the howls of the screechers, and the roars they made as they mutated into Beasts. My dad heard them too. He stepped back. 'If you're going to save your grandmother, then I suggest you get a move...'

Down on the ground, the Beast's body was completely still. 'Oh,' my dad said. 'Whoops. It seems I've kept you talking too long. Still,' he shrugged, gesturing to the whole of her twisted, malformed body, 'I'm sure it's what she would've wanted.'

'N-nan?' I said, my voice hoarse and my throat tight.

Beside me, Ameena sat down in the snow. Her eyes were staring and her expression was blank. Her lips moved, but I couldn't hear anything of what she was saying.

A red mist of rage fell over me and I felt the sparks begin to race in anticipation. I swallowed hard and tried to remember how to breathe. 'I know what you're doing,' I croaked. 'But it won't work. You want me to use my abilities to attack you, b-but I won't. I won't let you win.'

My dad glared at me. I met his gaze and held it, not flinching, not letting him see how close I was to losing control.

'Fair enough,' he said, at last. 'It was worth a go, though, right? Can't blame your old man for trying. But you win, son. You win. I'll go, and I'll leave you in peace.'

He turned and began to walk away. I felt my heart race. I'd done it! I'd beaten—

'Oh, just one thing before I do,' he said. He turned back to face me and I saw he was holding the portable tape recorder in his hand. 'You asked me about this earlier. Would you like to hear it?'

I hesitated. 'What is it?'

'Only one way to find out,' he said. His thumb pushed down on the play button, and the sounds of chaos flooded out. It was just a noise to begin with, a big collective din that made no sense to my ears.

After a moment, though, I began to pick out individual sounds. Screams. Shouts. And the *beep-beep-beep* of a life support machine.

'...protect the patient!' a male voice barked. 'Don't let him...'

'...got a gun,' a woman screamed. 'For God's sake, somebody—'

BANG!

I jumped as the sound of a gunshot blasted from the tinny speaker.

'No, no, no!' wailed the male voice. 'Jesus Christ, someone help—'

BANG!

The tape went silent, aside from the beeping of the hospital machine. Then there came another sound. A voice. My dad's voice.

'Fiona,' he said softly. 'Fiona, wake up.'

My whole body tensed at the sound of my mum's name. My eyes went from the tape to his face. He winked at me and grinned his shark grin.

'Fiona,' the voice on the tape said again. 'It's time to get up now.'

There came a murmur, soft and faint, and the beeping of the machine became faster.

'That's my girl,' my dad's voice continued. 'Open your eyes now. Open your—'

On the tape, I heard my mum groan. Her voice, when it came, was frail and weak, but I'd have recognised it anywhere.

'Wh-where am I?'

'Look at me, Fiona. Look at me.'

I heard her let out a sharp gasp.

'N-no,' she begged. 'Please, no, don—'

BANG!

Once again, the tape went silent. For a moment, there was only the sound of the cassette's wheels squeaking around, and then he switched the machine off, and there wasn't even that.

I tried to scream, but no sound would come out. The sparks raged through me and the tape recorder exploded in his hand. He cried out in pain, but his face was twisted into an expression of demented delight.

'Ooh, that's it, son! That's my boy! Punish me, make me pay for what I've done!' He held his arms out wide and his whole body became engulfed by shadow. 'Only thing is, you're going to have to catch me first.'

And with that, he was gone, retreating to the Darkest Corners where I had no powers, no abilities with which to protect myself.

But I didn't care.

Ameena hadn't moved. She was slumped in the snow, still staring blankly ahead. 'Look after her,' I told Billy in a voice that sounded nothing like my own. It wasn't one voice at all, it was a hundred thousand voices, all talking at once, as if every one of the sparks were speaking alongside me.

He had killed her. *He had killed her right there in her hospital bed.*

I focused on a spark. The world around me became hazy and indistinct as I plunged myself into hell.

He had killed her. He had killed my mum. And that meant only one thing.

I was going to kill *him*.

Whatever the consequences.